D1500320

Rainbow Jordan

ALICE CHILDRESS
Rainbow Jordan

COWARD, McCANN & GEOGHEGAN, INC.
NEW YORK

Library of Congress Cataloging in Publication Data
Childress, Alice.
Rainbow Jordan and company.
SUMMARY: Her mother, her foster guardian, and
14-year-old Rainbow comment on the state of things
as she prepares to return to a foster home for yet
another stay.
[1. Foster home care—Fiction. 2. Mothers and
daughters—Fiction. 3. Afro-Americans—Fiction]
I. Title.
PZ7.C4412Rai   [Fic]   81-596
ISBN 0-698-20531-6   AACRI

First printing
Designed by Catherine Stock
Printed in the United States of America

To those being raised
by other than their natural parents—
because I have shared your experience—
and to all who care about us.

The author

1. RAINBOW

I'm standin here ready to go. The apartment got a dispossess notice on the door. Gas and light is turned off.
The fridge is like defrosted, okay? I dumped the spoiled
food . . . one lemon and a moldy bread. Social Service
say we won't be put out. There will be a court hearin to
halt eviction. Goody for that. Social Service not to
blame. But I'm not gonna talk against my own mother
and say she abandon me; not even to save our apartment.
Truth is, what else is it but *abandon* when she walk out
with a boyfriend, promise to come home soon, then
don't show? That's a drag. Talk bout feelin bad, I hate
when night is over. Each day I gotta wake up, face everybody and think up new lies.

There's school. They lookin for a parent to show. I've
hollered "She's sick" so many times till I can't pull that
one again. My soul is hurtin. I got a paper comin due
on "The Romance of English Literature," another on
"The Presidential Office and the Electoral College."
However, all that can be looked up in the library. There's
also a extra bonus score for the research. One paper I
once got a B-plus was "Accomplishments of Black People

in America"—I got the bonus for research. Wrote a gal-
lopin paper because I found lots of books on accomplishments. I told how Benjamin Banneker was a good sci-
entist and also help lay out the plan for Washington,
D.C. Told bout George Washington Carver and discoveries he made to put the peanut to use; made oil, face
powder and gangs of other products. He discovered the
same for the sweet potato . . . and *gave* it all to America.
He did not copyright his discoveries to make money. He
gave it as a Christian act . . . also, I guess, he mighta
thought the act would make white folks respect us and
be grateful. I named many accomplishers, right on up
to today . . . all kindsa Black celebrities . . . even Black
millionaires.

I also got me a B on a paper bout "The Black Family"—I told bout Martin Luther King, Jr., and his wife
and children, bout Medgar Evers and a boss line-a beautiful Black families. Some were not so well known, but
still fine, fine, fine. Now, I'm standin here and nobody
to talk to but me, myself and I. Black ball players and
movie stars just truly fine . . . but they can't pay our
rent. We gotta find some money. That's all my mother
is away trying to do—find us some money.

I am lonesome so regular till it's like a job I gotta
report to every day. Miss Josie, the lady I'm to go stay
with again, got a old 78 rpm record . . . "Heartaches."
Tell me about it! My guy, Eljay, is not much help. He's
kinda like almost my steady. No one is close enough for
me to tell bout my mother.

Miss Josie, she's okay but she's fifty . . . and always
boastin about it. No way I can talk my feelins to a "fifty."
But I do better with her than talkin with my mother,

who is twenty-nine, while I'm now fourteen. I look nearly old as she does, also carryin a few more pounds than I need, wearin a thirty-six-B-cup bra; standin almost as tall as her. My mother taught me to call her by first name. . . Kathie for Katherine. I spend a lot of time tryin to take care of us, keep our business to ourselves. She's size ten, lookin like a model . . . and hair longer than mine. Life is complicated. I love her even now while I'm puttin her down.

Right off, not long after I was born, she broke up with Daddy. He wasn't but sixteen noway. His name is Leroy Jordan. I never really had a *mama* and a *daddy*. I got a Kathie and a Leroy. He'd come see us off and on. I like Leroy very much and remember him. I liked him every time I saw him. He has a nice face. Kathie wasn't too tough bout seein him cause she wanted to hold on to our check, Aid to Dependent Children. "Get lost, Leroy," Kathie say. "You'll keep me from collectin Rainbow's A.D.C. Child is only four, so give us a break. After all, you good for nothin but lookin fine and gettin nowhere."

Kathie picked my name, "Rainbow." She say it sound like pretty colors and also people tell how there's a pot-a gold at the end. In school and on the block, I been teased bout that name "Rainbow." I now ask people to call me "Rainey" and tell them it is short for "Laraine." Rainey is a cool kinda name. Rainbow sound square and countrified.

I don't have me a grandmother. She died when Kathie was born. Kathie's aunt raised and took care of her till she died and couldn't do it anymore. Sometime things go that way.

Round our neighborhood, I got to know all the ladies who take care of children while the mothers go off to work. I fast changed from one to another cause we'd fall behind in payment and not catch up. Kathie smile pretty and laugh so fine till people always carry her tab longer than most. But, after all, they can't do it forever. When she won out and got A.D.C. payments it was a help cause she told me she needed money to look for a job. Kathie isn't educated enough to get a big thing goin but she is too smart to be contented with nothin. My mother gets boyfriends like jam draws flies. None ever was rich or well-off. When she was seventeen she got started as a part-time go-go dancer . . . giggin. A gig is a one-time job and not a steady thing. Lotta weekends she'd get to go-go with a giggin band, go outta town with them and play a club date. Kathie say her go-go is "moonlight money" to add to her job when she's workin or to her unemployment check and A.D.C.—our Aid to Dependent Children.

Kathie is a good dancer and never had lessons. She just play records and dance. When people be dancin on television she can do it right along with them. See a step one time and then she got it and gone.

When Kathie get in from a go-go gig she sometime bring in a ice-cream pack and some musician boyfriend to laugh and talk with us. She'd pay the babysitter, then wake me up to eat ice cream while they play records low so's not to bug people in the apartment next door.

This apartment is a cute place to live. Better than the one we had upstairs that was burned out when I was little. Last year I help Kathie put up this wallpaper. Flowers look like bells turned downside up. We did the livin room and the hall. We made a mistake. Hung one strip upside down with bells turn the other way. "Damn if I'm goin through any changes," Kathie say. So this how it stayed. She makes jokes bout "that's how life gets turn around while we not noticin." When she say that I stand on my head and say, "Do like this and you'll see it straight." She crack up laughin. I'd be glad I was makin her happy.

Some days my mother get mad for no reason a-tall. She just wake up mad and fuss all day long.

"Girl, I'm sick-a you. Shut up and don't ask me nothin!"

I know how to back off and keep my distance. One time, when I was little, she hit me so hard till I got a black-and-blue on my arm and shoulder. Just pounded on me and mad as the devil. Well, I had done wrong. Drank milk from the container without askin. She had plans for us to use that milk next day.

"I'm gonna beat all the black off you, Rainbow! You gettin fatter and greedier by the minute! Can't keep food in this house without you swallowin it down! Come here so I can knock hell out of you again!"

I wouldn't go to her. She had to catch me. I ducked behind chairs, tables, and lock myself in the bathroom while she scream on the other side of the door.

"I'm gon kill you! Wasn't for you I'd be somewhere. No man ever get serious . . . cause I got you! Damn stupid, greedy girl who don't know how to act!"

Next day was like nothin happen. Kathie kissin me, bakin a cake and makin me eat nearly all of it. When the A.D.C. check came she bought me pair-a black patent-leather sandals with matchin shoulder-strap bag.

Some of the best presents I ever got was the day after a beatin. Truth is she was not beatin on me every minute. Sure wouldn't hear bout any outsider givin me a bad time. One Sunday mornin she went downstairs and cussed a neighbor for screamin at me bout playin in the hall. Woman was scared. Kathie promised to knock her down if she ever pick on me again.

"You old witch! Where else she gonna play? Want her out in the street with trucks and bicycles?"

After that my mother warn me, "You stay out the public hallway and keep your backside in this house. Don't make trouble!" "Yes, Kathie," I say. I was proud cause she took up for me, also shame cause she was so loud. Heard by all the neighbors.

I'm standin here ready to go, waitin for Mayola, our caseworker. I don't wanta go, not even to Miss Josephine's. I rather be stayin with my own mother in our apartment, no matter how perfect anybody else might be. Truth be told, I *can't* stay with her if she drops out and nobody know where she's at. I could stay and take care-a myself, like I do when she's home, but fourteen is call "minor." So whatcha gonna do?

2. JOSEPHINE

I must be out of my mind. Why do I trap myself? I've had twenty children during the last two years, plus one repeater. What made me offer myself as an "Interim Home"? The money helps but not very much. Hal and I not having children could be the main reason. TV commercials did help my decision. Turn on the set and there's a flood of babies, toddlers and cute five-year-olds . . . they're selling soft drinks, real estate and whatever else. I enjoy the commercials. The regular program is nothing but axe murders and ghost stories. Maybe it was watching little ones in commercials that made me long for the patter of little feet; kiddies to say cute things and love like they were our very own.

I had two miscarriages a long time ago. Well, I can miscarry plans in more ways than one. The agency did not comb through TV commercials to select children for short-term care. They did not send sweet toddlers to gaze up at us with innocent eyes. They brought big, bad, sassy thirteen- and fourteen-year-olds . . . even older. They also have sullen ones. Some were pot-smokers. Rainbow Jordan, my repeater, is fourteen and tall enough to look me eye to eye. Not directly rude but walks around with her nose slightly in the air . . . as if she's superior and is merely allowing me to handle her situation. She is a definite case of child-neglect but puts on like it's all some kind of misunderstanding. Every once in a while her mother runs off with a boyfriend, not the same one, of course. The woman's only twenty-nine and looks like a child herself. If it wasn't for *the pill* she'd be walking out on twelve kids instead of one.

The child gets her arrogance straight from the mother. When Kathie does show up after a "temporary" absence, she sits . . . cigarette in hand, legs crossed, dress hiked up to the center-fold. Acts like she's been off to Paris and left Rainbow behind in a finishing school.

"And how's my girl been doin? Hope she didn't give any trouble. Rainbow, honey, straighten your stockins and tell me why you're wearin a earring in your nose."

"Oh, Kathie, my friend Beryl pierced her nostril and stuck a diamond in it."

"Well, we don't have any diamonds to stick in yours. Two holes is enough for a nose, why you need three?"

"Mine is not pierced. It's just a gold-fill, clip-on earring."

"Girl, that finish will wear off and make a sore. Take it off."

"Aw, Mother."

"Another thing, drop that 'Mother' and stick with *Kathie*. After all, thirty candles bout to light up my next birthday cake. I don't need you hollerin 'mama' while I'm still lookin for a new husband rollin in money. Keep growin fast like you do. . . . people be thinkin I'm forty."

"I'm not gonna grow any more. I measured most every day and I'm still the same."

The two of them grinned, neither one looking like a television commercial.

"Rainbow, honey, you can grow taller if you first lose weight, then you can be a fashion model."

The mother looks like "the lost girl" out of a TV show about crime and prostitution. A yard of wig hangs down her back to the hip. Her mouth forever shining with lipstick looking like a hemorrhage. Dress front cut down a half inch short of showing her navel. The navel must be deformed or else she'd show that. Rainbow couldn't wait to get packed and go home. But Mama was in no hurry. Lingered long enough to lay out a story for us . . . just as she had for the social worker.

"I had called where Rainbow's father lives and left word for him to send a telegram money order so she could pay rent, buy food and pay a sitter. After all, I knew I was gonna be delayed. . . ."

What was the delay? Another man in a scroungy hotel room? Mean thought. I'm jealous. The girl is always glad to go back, no matter what. I give the best of myself . . . and she's ever ready to leave. Once I made two dresses for her even though I had to delay delivery of a suit to my best customer . . . my best client. Here, for the first time in life, Rainbow had dinner by candlelight. Another evening here . . . she couldn't or wouldn't say grace. I showed her the blessing taught me by my Quaker neighbor, Rachel. We silently held hands, bowed our heads and "centered down," the Quaker way of meditation. Rainbow likes "centering down." Kathie returns . . . so many things gained get forgotten . . . she is only centered on watching her mother.

"That simple-ass, Leroy. As far away as he's been these

ten years . . . one thing he most always will do is keep
his word."

"Yeah, Ma . . . Kathie, like when I needed school
notebooks and spring-back binders. . . ."

"Uh-huh, he sent twenty-five dollars in the nick-a
time, like he promise. Sometime he forget and blow his
bread. When it's like that he send later stead-a right off.
Other times he think I'm jivin bout bein broke. He will
back up and pull stubborn. He know if things be tight
for true . . . I'll put Rainbow on collect call all over
Detroit and keep it goin till we get some action. One
thing I say in his simple-ass favor, even from another
state he will send us some bread sometime. Once he
sent two hundred dollars when he hit the figure for half-
a grand. We didn't even know he hit and nobody asked
him for boo!"

"Yeah, Kathie, you bought me a tan Easter coat and
bone-color shoes and bag."

"Some-a these emergency visits with you is also Rainbow's fault. She know how to read and write. Girl, why
don't you get on the case and write Leroy to send
money?"

"I did last time you was outta town. Letter came back
stamped he had moved. It say 'addressee unknown.' He
moved one time before and got a new phone number."

"Girl, nobody be perfect twenty-four hours round the
clock. After all. That's your father."

I think of the day Hal came in and saw Rainbow Jordan sitting by the living room window, dim evening light
shadowing her face. He laughed about it after she went
to bed. "Is that young woman our new 'interim child'?"

That was the evening he turned away when I stroked

his cheek and tried to kiss him. There is a first time of turning away . . . Well, we all have our days.

"Harold, *children* are any age under eighteen. Looks like most of them in need are the older ones."

Unlike him . . . irritable with me about nothing. He frowned and shook his head . . . the slight sprinkling of gray in his hair . . . shining. "Josie, is this 'the little one' you thought might cheer our Christmas? Do you plan to hang up her stocking? It may be large enough for Santa to leave a Ferrari in it. Do you plan to tell her the story of the nativity? Shall we sing carols and crack walnuts while decorating the tree? How about the plan to get up on Christmas 'morn' and open toys?"

He had seemed glad about the children, at first. It's wearing thin now. Slowly, ever so slowly he is changing. Goes out early and comes in late. He looks past my eyes. There's been less loving. In the morning, before shaving, he used to brush his cheek against mine . . . "Good morning, darkness, here's a sandpaper kiss." It's been a long while. One morning I reached for the sandpaper caress. He said, "Don't do that, Josie, I haven't shaved."

I tried to make light of his remark about the girl. I resented him taking out feelings about me on someone else. "She has never been able to be a child . . . according to her caseworker. Let's make a nice holiday for her."

He examined his fingernails for a moment and then there was his old brightness. "Let's do that!"

I've had Rainbow here several times and she always greets Kathie's return as though the woman has done no wrong. Talk about love and forgiveness. Daughter never asks mother questions. On the last visit, she fastened her suitcase with trembling hands while Kathie had another beer . . . as usual, explaining her absence with grand gestures, surveying fingernail polish, crossing and re-crossing her legs. I thought about Rainbow's little "boyfriend," Eljay . . . wondering how long it would be before they land in each other's arms and start the cycle over again . . . children having children. Eljay is a show-off. He walks with a bounce and a strut, like he's danc-ing. He *is* dancing and forever carrying one of those over-sized music boxes. It blares your head off. I believe people in Russia must be able to snap their fingers to his beat. The first time he visited, my lampshade quivered with music before I opened the door. His voice grumbles bass. "Rainbow home?"

No "Good day" . . . not even a "Hi" . . . just "Rainbow home?"

Now I'm waiting for her again. I tried to tell Mayola *no*. Just could not do it. I don't really want to see anyone but Harold. He's dropping in and out almost as often as Kathie Jordan. There's no caseworker to take me on until my "interim problem" is solved. I feel unloved these days . . . but that's none of Rainbow's concern. She will play reluctant house guest and I'll play willing hostess. When the children are delivered I always open my arms wide . . . "Just look who's here!" . . . and give a hug. People need to be hugged . . . even when they won't hug back.

3. KATHIE

Bein stranded outta town gives time to think. This hotel room gettin tiresome. Burke is snorin. I hope he keeps sleepin so I can get my head together, get my life lined up . . . and figure the next move. I'm tired-a bein a "case." People busy tellin me what to do and how to live. My nerves stay shook. Best I can do is what I'm doin. If I burn a dress with a hot iron, I can throw it away if it can't be fixed. But you gotta live forever with other mistakes. If I had a dollar for every time I goofed . . . I could buy a Cadillac, cash on the line.

One mistake I have to look at each and every day is my daughter, Rainbow; the other I telephone now and then . . . my ex-husband, Leroy. Fifteen was too young for me to have a child. Mother nature made me able to give birth from the age of twelve . . . but she didn't bother to turn my mind on the same year; strange, weird, crazy. Leroy did not need to be a father at sixteen. When he took Rainbow out . . . somebody always ask, "Whose baby is that?" I told him he better learn to wipe that stupid, young, simple-ass look off his face and learn to act like a man. The two of us took Rainbow to the Baby

Health Station for her checkup. The girl on the desk, lookin dead at us, say, "Where are the child's parents?" Me, I stop wearin hair braids and made him get outta those funky-lookin sneakers and the T-shirt sayin "The Best in Town." I grew up fast while he was still playin stickball in the street. Playin stickball with his cap turn backwards. What kind-a simple-ass way is that? His folks didn't want us to get married and neither did mine . . . but Rainbow was a fact and we all got a thing bout "honor" and doin right by the unborn.

"You and Leroy gonna be married if yall don't stay together but a hot minute."

That's what my aunt said. A year went by just like a minute. The two of us didn't do much but get on each other's nerves. He wasn't exactly a drag. Leroy use to crack me up with his talk and when we got hold-a some money we knew how to party. Use to buy jug wine, potato chips and pretzels and pack the one room/kitchenette with friends and well-wishers. He was popular and people could dig him. When we walk out together there was no silence where he pass.

"Hey there, Leroy!"

"My man, whatcha say?"

"Take it easy, dad."

"Whatcha know?"

"Where you been?"

"What's new?"

"Where you headed?"

"What's happenin?"

He just shrug his shoulders and wave like he was some ace baseball player, man of the year on a winnin team. His walk maybe was what got us in trouble. He didn't hop along like the imitation cats. He stand straight up and down with his shoulders squared back and his arms loose-like, hangin by his sides. When he'd pass by his boons they'd throw up their hands like for a make-believe fight and he would put up his guard and left jab so fast they'd back away laughin . . . sayin, "Man, you too much." And he was. Gettin nowhere but part-time deliverin groceries on Friday and Saturday and wouldn't go to school anymore.

He moved in with me and my sick aunt. Things never go down for me, like in a feature movie. Leroy was too *biggety*, wouldn't go to see bout welfare or even the Aid to Dependent Children. I put up my hair and my age and worked part time at the corner hamburger joint. Nothin to it but a counter and two tables. The owner, a young cat, was also takin in numbers. I kept my eyes open and my mouth shut and didn't hit a lick on that gamblin scene. Did nothin but serve counter, wait table and mind my business. Boss wasn't the worst except always pat my behind when he'd pass. Also he would sorta hit on me, sayin what a help a man could be to an understandin girl. He was married and separated, also had a girlfriend, dark brown with bleach blond hair. Wore red nail polish, look like shiny sequins mix in it. Had a boss figure and gorgeous big eyes. She use them too . . . would sit on the stool at the counter, them eyes coverin everything in sight, me, him, the menu, the customers, back of the place, the front and right on out to the sidewalk. She'd eyeball the joint every few minutes; repeat that performance like maybe somethin mighta changed since the last once-over. She was one old-lookin twenty-two, like she'd been here for a hundred

years and had to eyeball things to keep them lined up
like they oughta be. She work somewhere else, doin I
don't know what, but it allowed her time to drop in
unexpected to eye out the happenins. I had sense enough
to be scared-a her. Told her one day, "You don't have
to worry bout me. I'm married, have a child and a husband." She gave me a big toothy, quiet smile.

"I'm not worried bout you, honey. Fact is, I don't
worry. Anything bothers me, I fast take care of it."

He was scared-a her more than I was. Scared is un-
pleasant; so I left and served a little time on the five-and-
dime refreshment counter. People round here charged
so much money to take care-a Rainbow till there was
damn small profit in workin. But she was a cute baby.
And could go through milk! Sometimes Leroy bought
milk, other days I did, but damn if it wouldn't always be
gone. Look like babies got one thought, that's to empty
bottles on one end and wet Pampers on the other. She'd
use those Pampers box after box. Growin outta clothes
was another thing. I bought her sweater and bonnet sets
in bigger sizes, but in no time flat the sleeves wouldn't
even cover her wrists.

After I lost my aunt I knew me and Leroy were headin
for Quit Street. He could act biggety but too shamed to
go with me to Social Services. One thing he was, probably still is . . . good-lookin. His hair is crinkly wavy and
face smooth as silk, had a fine mustache before the other
boys could grow six hairs. His lips ruddy brown and just
a little bit full like African pictures of warriors. Leroy's
eyes deepset and dark. When he smile who could believe
it? Like somebody turn on lamp-light in a dark room.
His laugh and his talk sound so sexy, like sayin "I love

you" even though might be givin you the football score.
Just had us one year before the spark went out. Every
girl in junior high seemed to want Leroy, but I was the
one got him. Oh, well, love just wore out. Too much
was on me and he had nothin else to do but turn jealous
bout fellas in places I worked. Damn, at least I was workin, more than you could say for him. He was childish.
Thinkin every guy in the world was after me. Course,
some of them was, but not *every*body.

He didn't like it when I got me a natural bush hair
style, flipped when I had it process, then blew his top
cause I bought a Eva Gabor wig. Nothin I did was ever
right. I told him.

"I gotta look good out here searchin for work. I can't
face the public like I'm havin a hard time."

"Kathie, that's how come you don't last on a job. Why
go round seemin like outta *Playboy* magazine?"

"How long you lasted on a job? You deliverin groceries
lookin fine as O. J. Simpson! Leroy Jordan, you so sharp
till people fraid to tip you. They be thinkin maybe you
posin as 'delivery' but really front man for *Candid Camera*."

"All I'm sayin, mouth-mama, is for you to buy the
baby milk stead-a blowin bread on some wig."

"Oh, yeah? Why don't you quit smokin and get milk
with that? Another thing, stop payin nine bucks for a
high-style haircut and buy even more milk!"

Just turn into nag, nag, nag. His people move out to
Detroit, then he start mumblin bout movin out to give
it a try. I push him to go on do it. Nothin was goin for
him here. I know I didn't go. I haven't lost anything in
Detroit. We knew it was over, without sayin. Hard to

remember how one time I was crazy in love with Leroy.
Used to be like I ached inside whenever he was outta my
sight. Every night I prayed for one thing to be mine
. . . Leroy. If a day went by without me seein him . . .
I'd go off and be alone so I could remember his face
without anybody stoppin my remembrance by a word or
a question. When I wasn't near him I was alone, alone,
alone. No one else would do. I didn't even wanta eat or
sleep . . . cause anything I did was takin time out from
thinkin bout him. Who would believe such love could
go dead? We had a farewell pizza and a cola . . . was
jokin kinda bout how we were gonna soon hit it rich, go
back together, send Rainbow to private school, buy us
a foreign sport car . . . and like that. But we knew.
Sometime over is over.

He's not the worst, sends little piece-a money now
and then. I still say that's not bad for someone who is
states away . . . out of our court jurisdiction.

Glad I still get Rainbow's A.D.C. Those checks come
in handy. Good luck does not follow my footsteps too
tough. I've had trouble with men, one after another. I'm
not lookin for a screamin millionaire, but look like
nothin is shakin. Money has more than a little to do
with happy-ever-after. People tell me I'm pretty, so what?
Can't walk to the corner without some guy whistlin.
Never been to a party where I'm not the popular one.
So what? Some people think bein pretty makes life
groovy. Others think pretty girls gotta be prostitutes . . .
or else oughta be. One fella tried to fast-talk me into that
. . . after pretendin he could get me a job.

"Kathie, baby, why not make your good looks pay?"
"Pay like how?"

"Lotsa guys be willin to cough up big money for a fast half-hour of your company . . . could be fifteen minutes."

Me, fool that I am, I had been thinkin he wanted me to have and to hold, to take care of in this cruel world. But he wasn't nothin but ready to send me out to lie down with any stranger that happen to have money. It hurt my feelins. He was not good at readin feelins.

"Baby, hookin ain't nothin but a business, like any other. You don't have to walk the street . . . there are smooth ways to go bout the thing. Like bein call girl for only the high-class customers."

"That sound too much like old-time slavery days. I gotta do what 'Massa' say cause he's the one with the money."

"That's also true if you washin dishes for somebody . . . or sweatin your days out in a factory."

"I'm not interested in bein a hooker no matter how fine you explain it, okay?"

Fella's face tightened up cold as ice. For a second I thought he was gonna throw me a fist. He didn't . . . started givin me the exit business, windin his watch and mumblin how he had to make a "quick run." He tried to perk up some. "Gimmie a call if you ever have any *real* talk for me." He threw small change on the counter . . . to pay the bartender for my beer, walked off and left. The bartender was like laughin at a secret joke. I'm not sure if the joke was on me or the fella. I'll never forget that weird night.

Rainbow was then five. I had spent the babysitter money and bought her two pair-a cute pajamas, kind with feet so her toes would be warm if she kicked off the

covers like she always do. Also had bought new black
patent shoes with a ankle strap . . . like she had been
wantin. Yes, I HAD LEFT HER ALONE. I had been
bein so damn good till life was like no fun a-tall. Gotta
go out sometime. I told her not to open the door for
anybody, not to play with matches or to light the stove.
Gave her a bubble bath and nice hot cereal. That fella
had been after me to go out with him and kept sayin
how he could help me. People lose interest if you never
can go anywhere. He was a louse.

I walked home from the bar real slow. Savin carfare
was only part-a the reason; I wanted to breathe cool night
air and clear my head of that cruddy creep. Before I got
to our corner . . . I knew. Fire engines, smoke, crowds
and noise . . . FIRE. Next thing you be hopin it's not
where you live. But that's the side-a the street that was
blocked off. . . . Mine. It was my floor and one above
and one below. I fell right down on the ground screamin
her name . . . Rainbow! Rainbow! Rainbow!

The law took me to the police station and put me
through a child-neglect charge . . . like some criminal.
Rainbow was there, alive and well, eatin a ice-cream
cone and still wearin her new pajamas . . . smoky and
dirty as a imp outta hell. I was glad . . . also mad.

"Thought I told you not to play with matches?"

"I didn't do nothin, Kathie."

She hadn't. Some cheap-ass wirin in the wall had
caught fire without anybody doin anything. That's how
come I was put on probation by a judge. I had to report
to court regular concerning her welfare and like that.
What almost broke me down was how they took my own
child away from me and put her in a "temporary home"

with *strangers*. The court said I had to "prove myself"
and make a proper home. Gave me "visitin rights." Lotta
crap. But nobody can hold me down forever. Soon as
that buildin was repair and passin the fire laws . . . I got
in another apartment. It's been fixed up with wallpaper
and pin-backs on the curtain. My daughter help me to
decorate. I dead sure got her back with me where she
belong and wanta be. We been stayin one place steady.
I wasn't tryin to prove nothin. I *want* the best for her.
Mayola and Social Services can run their mouth . . . I
run my life. But I do not want this fella *Burke* to mess
up for me. He can't make me stay in a motel room
forever. I'm layin back thinkin while he sleeps. I'm linin
it up . . . takin care-a business.

4. RAINBOW

"A penny for your thoughts."

That's what Mayola just said. Social workers don't know what they be askin. Wish we would just leave so she could double lock the outside door . . . if we goin. I'm thinkin I'd stay right here and take care-a myself if they'd turn that A.D.C. check over to me. Fourteen is too old to still be counted a legal *child* . . . with a stranger in charge. Not that Miss Josie is a stranger. In a way, I wish she was. This my third stay comin up and it's gettin harder for me to keep her from seein how Kathie keeps goofin. The other times could be like slip-ups . . . but it's tough to laugh off number three.

"Nothin much, Miss Mayola, I'm not thinkin any-thing."

Mayola now go to signifyin how I might *like* her to look up Kathie's second cousin, Aurelia. She live down in Georgia. I never met her and she hardly even knows my mother a-tall. No way is she close. One Christmas she sent a over-size Christmas card sayin . . . THE SAV-IOR WAS BORN TO SAVE SINNERS . . . She was usin the card to hit at Kathie. Kathie wised me to her. She say that same cousin once was goin with her own sister's husband . . . while she also was married to one of her own. Look to me like she'd be sendin cards to herself. Kathie will return like always . . . so there's no need for Social Services to look up any cousins. Mayola don't mean harm. Sometime her eyes go misty and she pat my shoulder. I told her.

"That cousin. She'd be a stranger to me. I . . . I'd rather be with Miss Josephine for a short visit."

If money didn't run out, we wouldn't have to trouble people when Kathie go off the way she do. Mayola say how some rich folk leave their children for a long time but there's a maid with them or they be goin to camps or sleep-in schools . . . and like that. Our apartment look good for bein three rooms. We sent away mail order for the dress closet. Have to slide it open. It's paperboard, will buckle if you pull the door . . . gotta slide it easy. We covered it to match our wallpaper. It gives extra closet space.

"Rainbow, I'm checkin out gas jets and water faucets before we leave. Don't worry . . . we'll think up solutions."

"Yes, mam."

Mayola is okay but I wish she wouldn't think solutions. I close the extra closet careful-like. Kathie got more clothes than me, that's cause she's easier to fit. She wear "Honey Buns" jeans. Got "Honey Buns" stitch on the back pocket. Bought it mark down for twenty dollars, they go for *sixty*. She lives in jeans. "Honey Buns" her sharpest pair. They too tight for me. Chubby size is too large for me and regular is like too small. When I was bout eleven, Kathie came home with two blouses for me

. . . cute style but one was too big, the other too small.
It split under the arm. She got mad with me cause it was
no-exchange or refund, on clearance.
"Dammit, nothin fits you!"
The next week she bought yard material, patterns
. . . paid down on a credit sewin machine . . . and in
no time she learn herself to thread and operate it . . .
from the instruction book. She say, "I'm gonna be a
good mother if it kills me." Followed patterns and was
cuttin and sewin like mad.
"Kathie," I say. "Don'tcha wanta take my measure?"
She wave me off from botherin her. "Don't need to,
that's why I bought patterns." I was more chubby then
than now.
She kept steady sewin for two/three days, also went
through two six-packs-a beer. Sent me down the corner
to get number three.
"Kathie, they not gonna sell me beer or cigarettes. Say
I'm a minor."
"Get Jimmy to wait on you. He'll sell you a elephant
if you got money to buy it."
"Elephant maybe, but not beer."
"Girl, stop pokin out your mouth fore your lips stay
lookin like a country sausage. And stop walkin like a
wrestler. Soon's you get back, go take a bath fore the
board-a health send a inspector in here after you."
All of a sudden she stop frownin and then laugh. "You
all right, Rainbow. Buy a pint-a ice cream if you want.
I need some cold brew to stay at this machine. It may
be an up-to-date style but somebody still got to run it.
What we needin is a computer sewin machine so you
can tell it what to do and it'll go ahead and make a dress.

Computer sure knows how to send the electric, gas and telephone bill. Need some new kinds that'll sew, wash, iron and dust."

I tried to tell her. Jimmy would not sell me a six-pack. I bought the ice cream and went on back home. She had two cans inside of her and they told her to get up and take me back to the store. Turn out the whole place bout nothin.

"Look, Joker! Clown! You know Rainbow's mine and not here to buy for herself. It's for me! I'm workin hard and don't need a damn soul to make life any tougher!"

Sometime Kathie be loud and wrong. He sold it to *her* but not payin any mind about the arguin. Jimmy kept sayin, "Law is the law is the law." She went on fussin while pickin out two TV dinners for supper so she could finish sewin.

Stitchin went on steady till near midnight. I fell asleep durin the late show bout a woman who got her lover to kill off her third husband. Sure didn't mean to sleep through that. Kathie woke me up to try on my dresses. First didn't fit, second didn't and the next wouldn't even go over my shoulders cause no zipper to let down. She got mad and slap me so hard, with the dress still halfway over my head. I couldn't get my arms out. She hittin and hittin hard and screamin.

"Nothin fits you! What the hell is the matter? I do and I do and for what? Things always goin wrong with you! If you ain't tryin to burn yourself up in a fire you busy not fittin in new clothes! I'm sick-a you!"

I tried to run but couldn't see with the dress caught over my head. Bumpin into the dresser, fell over a chair. Nowhere else to go. I went fallin backward on the studio couch. "Please," I said, "stop! You killin me! Please, Kathie!"

She stop as fast as she start, was cryin and shove that sewin machine off the table. It banged to the floor. Sound like it was goin through to downstairs. Somebody next door knock on our wall. She cut that dress off me with a scissors, then was huggin me and cryin.

"I didn't mean to hurt you, honey."

"You didn't hurt me all that much, Kathie."

But it did hurt, put a mark on my cheek and one eye swollen. I stayed home from school. The next day she bathe my face in cool water and vinegar. Ask forgiveness and was cryin. I did forgive cause five of her six-pack was empty . . . and that's what made trouble. She kept the number-six can to start the next day with no headache. That's when the A.D.C. check came, that very next day. She let me stay home from school again . . . it was Friday anyway. We went to the check-cashin place, she paid to get it cash then we went shoppin and bought me a joggin suit. She let me pick out the color . . . blue with a green stripe. When she's not goofin, Kathie is okay.

Glad I'm fourteen and in ninth grade. Soon be time to graduate and go to regular high school . . . if I pass everything, make up papers due and finish remedial math. The best friends I once had have now move away. Parents all say cause "neighborhood is changin" . . . that's all you hear. I'm bout the last to stay on in my school and neighborhood. That's okay. I got two new friends . . . Eljay, my guy . . . and Beryl, who's almost like my best friend. They like me. I hate havin friends who move far away.

Mayola does not like me to be quiet. "Rainbow! I'm in the kitchen . . . writin a note to let your mother know where you are if . . . er . . . er . . . *when* she returns. Say somethin, honey, don't be so quiet."

"I'm okay, Miss Mayola, I'm cool."

5. RAINBOW

One thing not fair or true. Kathie always goin years back and sayin I tried to burn myself up when I was five. It was no fun to be left alone. Whenever she was dressin to go out I use to talk and talk. I didn't want her to leave. She did look so pretty. Every time she try on her go-go costume to see how it look in the mirror . . . even if she wasn't gonna dance . . . just be tryin it on, like for luck.

The night of the fire, I remember. Seem like some man knew somebody else who might hire her to work steady. The first man wanted to talk first. When Kathie moves . . . the fringe be swingin on her costume. These days she now got better-lookin costumes than she used to have. White satin panties and bra, with silvery fringe. Sometime she get pay seventy-five or a hundred dollars . . . just for havin a good time dancin. Trouble is . . . it's only now and then. She never like how some clubs want her to be bout naked. She won't. They had to let her alone cause people love her dance and the way the fringe be swingin. They also wanted her to sing as well as go-go, but she can't carry a tune nicely. Kathie say, "Honey, I'm livin proof that *all* of us can't sing." She laugh bout that.

I never tried to burn myself up. That's a unfair memory. She was goin to meet that first man who had promise a job. My mother so fine and pretty till look like anybody oughta gladly give her a break. She was happy bout goin out and sad cause my stomach hurt.

"Rainbow, you get a pain every time I'm bout to walk out the door. When I stay home nothin hurts. You want a candy bar?"

"Yeah!"

"See there? If you was really sick you wouldn't. Take that last Milky Way, eat it and stop talkin aches and pains."

A sitter used to come but she charge two dollars a hour and Kathie say that knock the profit out of our life. We need our money to buy stuff for ourselves. That night she made me say the rules out loud like always.

"I'm not to open the door for anybody. Don't play with matches. Don't light the stove. Don't open the window to look out. Don't watch any scary TV. Don't forget to turn off the set. Go to bed right after."

"That's my good girl."

I remember clearly . . . like it's this minute. When she went I watch TV to keep from hearin other sounds. All kindsa sounds happen when TV not runnin. Noises like floor creakin, somebody walkin upstairs, somethin in the bathroom. When I go look there's nothin there, but soon as I go back to bed, the sounds again. I hear people passin in the hall, sometime sayin bad words, sometime not. Can hear buses goin by at the corner. If I put my face against the window glass, see little bit of the corner and the bus lights passin. Lady down in the street was callin somebody . . . "Hoolio! Where you at?

Hoolie! Hoolio!" She call "Hoolio" every night. Under a street lamp cross the way . . . boys holler bad words and throwin pennies, fightin bout who's to pick up money.

A cop car come by makin a whoop-whoop noise . . . them boys runnin away fast. Lady stop callin "Hoolio." No more boys and bad words. It was quiet. I went to pee. Flush the toilet nicely. It keep on runnin water and flushin until I jiggle the handle, then it stop. Wash my hands with perfume soap, stood there smellin soap. Was careful not to splash and drop suds on my pretty pajamas.

It was a nice TV story. A man loves this lady but she not lovin him. They kissin each other anyway. Open her mouth so wide like she gonna eat him up. Man was gettin mad bout her lovin somebody else. He start thinkin bout killin her, lookin at his gun. Had to turn on another station. Killin can be scary. Other station even worse. A big, dark house, not enough light, just the moon shinin . . . window curtains blowin and a lady layin cross her bed . . . no light a-tall . . . a dog howlin. . . . had to turn that off.

I remember goin to the dresser to try on Kathie's new lipstick. Was hard to rub off. Blusher looks good on my cheeks. Washed it off with perfume soap, then smell the soap again. Got my Milky Way out the fridge. Ate it slow so it would last. Wiped chocolate off my hands with the washcloth, then wash the washcloth. Soap still smellin good. Got in bed, said "Our Father." Sunday school gave me a Easter basket for sayin it right. Never will forget. Children's program award.

When I woke up the room was smoky. Coughin and

coughin. Lotta screamin in the hall. I wouldn't open the door. Went to the front room, lights was shinin all over. A fireman on our fire escape peepin in the window. Pushed it up. . . .

"Anybody in there? Come on, hurry! Over here! Let's go."

First I went and got my new shoes. He came in, snatched me up and carried me down the fire escape. Upstairs smoke and fire poppin out of windows makin a lotta noise. People out in the street hollerin. I wondered which one was "Hoolio." Got a ride in a real police car. Wanted to wait for Kathie but they took me off. A lady asked a lotta questions bout if my mother left me alone other times. I didn't answer. Looked at the ceilin. Brushin smoke dust off my fine pajamas. Was hopin Kathie wouldn't get mad. I did not light any matches. Fire came from upstairs is what firemen said. They kept askin more. I kept right on sayin nothin. The lady shook her head. "Poor little thing is in shock."

Kathie cried when they took me away to the first "interim" home. Social worker said, "The Grahams are a stable Black family." The lady was nice, so was her husband and their two children. Boy name Arthur, girl was Lee-Ann. I had my own room. That part was good.

They were stable and also rich. Had a lady come once a week to dust and clean the two bathrooms. They also had two cars . . . and a Ping-Pong table in the basement play room. Once a month was "visitation day." Kathie missed the first one but made the next two. Social Services let her have me back . . . so we could be stable like other people. The Grahams smiled and waved good-bye to us. I believe they were glad to see me go. I had hit

Lee-Ann on the head with a Ping-Pong paddle ·⁛. . that very morning.

I never tried to set myself on fire. That's somethin Kathie says cause she's still mad bout bein arrested on child neglect. Well, that's the past. I wish I knew where she is now, if she's okay . . . and when she's comin back.

6. JOSEPHINE

The first time Rainbow entered my life she wasn't quite thirteen and not as hard to deal with as the ten-, eleven- and twelve-year-olds. Once they brought me a delightful boy of seven. He was bright, talkative and pleasant. In a few days relatives from out of state came to pick him up. His mother and father had been injured in a car crash. We wanted to keep him until his parents recovered. Another child we had was polite but tried to steal all he could see. Took money from my purse, Hal's pen set, and my gold-and-opal earrings. He'd wake up in the middle of the night to prowl through the house while we were asleep. His mother and father were being "held" for car theft. The boy must have brilliantly learned too much of the wrong thing. Before he left we searched his suitcase to find my perfume which I had not yet opened, also two cakes of strawberry soap. We lectured him about stealing. What we got for our pains was a wide-eyed look. Hal made him sit on a chair, wouldn't allow him to move except to visit the bathroom. We checked the medicine chest behind him and found he'd picked through that, took old toothbrushes, shaving

cream, *anything*. As aggravating as he was, I couldn't
help caring, that's why his ways distressed me so. Maybe
his new foster parents have done some good . . . if he
didn't steal all of their worldly goods. The caseworker
warned me, "Watch your pocketbook." When she came
back to pick him up I told her, "Don't watch your pocketbook, watch *him*." I don't see many good things ahead
for these wounded children. Foolish me, I thought I
could turn them around with kindness.

Rainbow is very independent. She had her first period
during our first interim visit. It was hard for her to tell
. . . a stranger. It was vacation time so fortunately did
not happen in school. It does for so many girls.

In my own case, long ago as it was, I can still remember going to the bathroom to stuff toilet paper in my
underwear. I couldn't make myself tell teacher. I would
have had to ask her to step out of the classroom, or else
whisper in her ear. There were also boys in the room.
I didn't know what else to do except constantly raise my
hand and ask permission to "leave the room."

"But this is the very last time, Josephine."

Somehow I managed to get home . . . soiled through.
My mother went to school next day to explain why I had
left without permission. She asked her out in the hall to
talk about it. Miss Bynum said, "The child should have
told me."

I couldn't, without making it public. No place for
privacy in a classroom. I have met great-grandmothers
who clearly remember their first menstrual period . . .
time, place and circumstance, it's never forgotten. Poor
Rainbow, that taking place while her mother was missing. She had to ask me for the fixings. Had no money

at the moment . . . but, more than that . . . she needed to tell someone.

On the second day she had to ask my help. Supplies and instructions are easily handed out . . . but menstruation is special. It calls for a talk between girl and a woman. It is difficult. I didn't call the caseworker. Too much like reporting. If there is one day in life when a girl should be with her mother . . . it is this "first." I tried to recall what my mother had said . . . not much . . . "This'll happen every month. Keep clean by shower. Don't sit in a tub bath until it's over." My mother tried not to look directly at me. I was uneasy, so was she. She stammered about not "playing with boys" . . . or getting into "trouble." I brought the subject to an end . . . to spare her strained feelings. "Yes, mam, I see, I know, that's right, yes'm."

I have to watch my step. Some parents don't want other people telling their children the facts of life. Nobody dares mention genitals. Some schools give "Sex Information" as part of physical ed. Some parents object. However, what if the child is visiting—living in an "interim" home? What if, like Rainbow, she also is suffering from cramps? I did the best I could. Why the devil was I scared of talking to a child?

"Rainbow, have you heard about menstruation? Do you know it will happen about every twenty-eight days?"

"Yes, mam."

"Did your mother tell you about it?"

"No, I heard from other people . . . my friends."

"Do . . . do you know what it means?"

"It means I'm old enough to have a baby."

"Well, do you know exactly how?"

"More or less. Sorry I had to bother you. I didn't have money to buy sanitary napkins, that's all."

"You're sure you never discussed this matter with Kathie?"

"We don't talk that stuff."

"This is a natural event, it is not a 'sickness' or a curse. You have an almost invisible egg in your womb. Nature has gathered nourishment in the form of blood . . . to nourish it . . . so it can grow into a baby if . . . if . . ."

"If it is fertilized by the male sperm."

"Well, that's right. Usually, in the case of a young girl, it is *not* fertilized and the entire contents of the womb is discarded . . . and then the whole procedure is repeated . . . unless fertilization . . . er . . . ah, pregnancy takes place. It is not a 'sickness' or a curse . . ."

"You said that."

But she looked at me with more interest. "I can now have a baby. That's a big thought."

"That is if the egg is er . . . fertilized by the entry of the . . . the sperm . . ."

"I *know* that. Why doesn't nature wait and start all of this *after* people get married?"

A good question. She is walking around with a time bomb, that egg waiting to be fertilized. Why doesn't nature wait until a girl is wearing her wedding dress? Wait until the preacher speaks over the bride and groom . . . "Now, dearly beloved, now you may multiply . . . give birth." Mother nature does start this motherhood possibility at a very early age . . . sometimes eleven or twelve. I started the bumbling conversation so. . . .

"Rainbow, if you had a daughter, how would you explain this?"

"Well, like I would say how it's happenin . . . like how what life is. Like you were just sayin, only I'd tell it more-so . . . like . . . like, Miss Josephine . . . like I really don't know offhand."

"For some reason it seems hard to explain. All I'm trying to say is you be extra careful . . . to remain a girl even when nature calls you 'woman.' "

She giggles and helps me out. "You mean don't get in trouble."

"Rainbow, I ask you to remember that we call some females 'unmarried mothers' . . . but I've never heard of an 'unmarried father.' There are 'homes' and 'shelters' for 'unwed mothers' . . . none have yet been set apart for 'unwed fathers.' Young girls are 'disgraced' but young boys are 'trapped.' "

The thought angers her. "Why does it stay that way? Is it cause girls are stupid and boys are free?"

"It's a time when nature shoves and pushes us around. We call it 'puberty,' 'coming of age.' It's a time when young people become more interested in each other . . . sexually. . . ."

"Go, you doin fine, Miss Josie."

". . . the young are now attracted to caring for each other, more than they care for their parents. Nature is pushing them to fall in love. Nature is selfish. Nature's job is to bring more and more people into the world. . . . I guess."

"You got it . . ."

"But man has invented civilization . . . that makes it possible for us to have comfortable houses, education, money. . . ."

"And so?"

"Look, Rainbow, use self-control. Don't let mother nature decide your future too soon. She'll take over and run you ragged. You have to let her know who's boss."

She asked for aspirin to ease cramps. An "interim" parent is not to give "unprescribed medication." I made weak tea with a dash of cinnamon in it. Served it in my favorite bone china cup. She sat there sipping sadly, my crewel cushions plumped all around her. Such a sweetly dark girl. She tried not to look pleased about being waited on . . . but loved it. She loves all special times . . . when I ran bathwater for her, when I pressed her ruffled blouse, when I made her a plaid skirt . . . all the many things I do that she's had to do for herself . . . or else do without.

"Miss Josephine, is there truly such a thing as a 'bad' girl? Are bad girls the ones who get in trouble . . . get pregnant? Sound so to me."

"Good and bad. How do you define that? Having a child should not be a disgrace . . . that's truth as I feel it . . . and yet . . . and yet . . ."

"Yeah, and yet what?"

"Once in a while, during school days . . . a few of us are lucky enough to run into a special teacher. Someone who brings sense to our lives. I remember a woman who was fired from teaching because she was secretly married."

"For real? You gotta be kiddin."

"It used to be that only single women could teach. Some married secretly to keep their jobs. A man could marry and teach . . . but it was considered *indecent* for a married woman to instruct children."

"So, what happened?"

"The principal came into the classroom, made my

teacher clear out her desk . . . fired her on the spot.
'You are a married woman! Unfit to teach children!' She
wept, cleaned out her desk and made ready to leave. I
cried. She was my favorite. The big sinner was *my* favorite. I wasn't sure what to think. Three o'clock, school
was over. Way down at the end of the street, on the
corner . . . was Miss Line, my favorite. My third-grade
teacher was waiting. I ran to her and told how I hated
the principal and didn't care if he thought I was 'unfit'
or not."
   "And what'd she say?"
   "She said . . . 'You are good, Josephine and so am I.
Here is one last assignment. There's a poem by a man
named Charles Kingsley. The title is . . . "A Farewell."
You find it in the library and memorize it. It goes . . .

> *My fairest child, I have no song to give you;*
> *No lark could pipe to skies so dull and gray:*
> *Yet, if you will, one quiet hint I'll leave you*
> *for every day.*
> *I'll tell you how to sing a clearer carol*
> *Than lark who hails the dawn on breezy down;*
> *To earn yourself a purer poet's laurel*
> *Than Shakespeare's crown*
> *Be good, sweet maid, and let who will be clever;*
> *Do noble things, not dream them all day long:*
> *And so make Life, and Death, and that For Ever*
> *One grand sweet song.' "*

   Rainbow forgot to sip her cinnamon tea. "Poor Miss
Line. I dig the poem except for 'My *fairest* child' . . .
Would be nicer if they also included us . . . like sayin
. . . 'My *darkest* child . . .' "
   "Well, Rainbow, 'fair' also means beautiful. I'm sure

he wanted everyone to like his poem."

"What happened to poor Miss Line and the no-good principal?"

"I never saw her again. That was a Jim Crow school, a school segregated by law. Miss Line and the principal had nothing to do with that and neither did I. At that time—none of *us* made laws."

"Principal didn't act right about it."

"We all thought we were right."

"But somebody was wrong."

"The law was wrong. The principal couldn't afford to know it . . . or maybe he believed it was right. It's not a law anymore. Now, that's all I can say about good and bad."

She looked thoughtful . . . more than when we started. All in all, perhaps it wasn't too bad that her womanhood took place where and when it did.

7. RAINBOW

I'm ready to again go back to Miss Josie. One last look around. Kathie can't say it was left a mess. Window curtains in place with butterfly pins holdin them neatly. Fridge defrosted. Clothes hung except for her housecoat over the back-a the chair. I'm leavin her slip-on house slippers on the floor. She might be tired when she get home. Always like her slippers and robe waitin out but nothin else pile on chairs, looking messy. Wish I could be here when she come back and see all this perfect neatness. She'll be back.

I never trusted Burke, this new boyfriend. Don't like him. He doesn't lose much time over me either.

When Burke walked in he took over. Put his feet up on the coffee table, rarin back like he's the big shot. Kathie say, "Put your feet on the floor, Burkie, less you plannin to buy a new table."

He pop his fingers, actin trashy. "Pretty mama, I'm gon buy you some-a everything they makin. Just wait till my ship come in." He got hot cause I ask—"Did you send one out?" Kathie made me say I was sorry bout bein rude. Said it, but wasn't sorry. Only sorry thing was I

didn't know he was behavin his *best* when talkin bout
ships comin in. One night he followed my mother home
from a go-go job and banged on the door, kept it up until
she had to open.

"Hey, cut that out. Rainbow is asleep. What's your
story?"

"I know you got another man! Who else in there?"

"None-a your damn business!"

He shove her to one side and walk on through. I woke
up and rubbin my eyes. He's eye-ballin the bed, lookin
underneath, also in my closet, the bathroom . . . and
even out on the fire escape. "If I catch you two-timin
me somebody's gon die!" he say.

"You a fool! What make you think some man is here?
You got no claim on me! I'm a married woman without
a divorce, okay? Why you gotta break bad? You not payin
my bills! Breakin my door down! I'll call the law!"

Burke is past six feet tall and heavy. He could snap
her in two if he gently pat her on the back. That old-
time Afro way he wears his hair make him look taller
than that. There's a big cut-glass pitcher on the dresser,
was my grandmother's. If he kept it up and go to put his
hands on Kathie I'd-a broke it right over his head . . .
hard. I'd-a part his Afro down the very middle. He was
sweatin like a rainstorm.

"Why you left the club? Didn't I say I'd be by to pick
you up?"

"You was late."

"If I say I be there, I be there! All you gotta do is wait,
woman!"

"Oh, you goin on bout nothin. What's wrong?"

Kathie was backin down. Her eyes not steady like always. Could see she was scared-a him. I hated him for scarin her. Sure got no business lookin under my bed and searchin.

All of a sudden he start *cryin*. "Woman, you *ever* walk out on me . . . I'll kill the both of us!"

Kathie's mouth went wide open. "Burke, you crazy?"

"Don't say that to me! Don't give no hard time. I know you likin the guitar player!"

"You must be drunk, all I can say."

Burke start rakin a Afro comb through his hair and studyin me. "Hey, Rainey, the guitar player been here?"

Mama ask, "Now you checkin on me? Tell him, honey, so we can have peace."

"Nobody been here."

He laugh and pull my hair. "You gon lie for her no matter what. But I take your word this time. Little puddin face, look like you tellin the truth."

Too bad *I* can't give advice. Kathie had been jumpin on me ever since she come home one afternoon and Eljay was here. He had walked me home. I fixed us peanut butter sandwiches and divided a soda. Fact is, Beryl had been there too, but she cut out to meet her guy at Teen Canteen Youth Center. We'd-a been there but I was told *not* to go without permission. I was doin nothin but right. She walked in and *flipped*. Eljay's jacket was on the couch and he was in the bathroom. I explained his jacket and told where he was. She put her hands on her hips. "What's he doin in my bathroom? That does *not* look nice. Boy in the bathroom when I come home." She gave him the deep freeze when he came out. Barely nodded when I introduced him, went to walkin from one room to the other, doin nothin in

particular. Eljay gave me the wink like he was on to her.
All of a sudden she sat down across from him and start
with cold questions.

"You live round here?"

"Uh-huh."

"Where?"

"Next block."

"You go to Rainbow's school?"

"Rainbow?"

I had told all the new kids they could call me *Rainey*
and that it stood for Laraine. Lotta kids have razz me
bout that *Rainbow*. Nobody in the world ever was name
that. Lotsa African names are in. One girl name *Olay-
inka*. That is *cool*. But whenever anybody say *Rainbow*
somebody else gotta crack up. One boy say, "You too
dark to be a Rainbow. They shoulda call you *Storm-
cloud*." Now everybody is more sayin *Rainey*, even the
teacher, cause I *ask* her to do it. When she call the roll
she now politely say . . . "Rainey Jordan?" Kathie had
to go and blow it.

Eljay slap his hands together. "Whoo! *Rainbow!* How
bout it!"

"Yes, that's my daughter's name."

She go on to worry him with questions bout his mother
and father. She also was gettin mad cause he wouldn't
tell but so much. I can't strong-arm *her* company like
that without havin to apologize. True, I'm the child and
she's the parent, but she could be cool and ask *me later*.
One thing, Eljay didn't get ruffled. Kathie say, "Is your
mother expectin you home?"

"No, and my father's not expectin me either. I'm goin
to canteen, watch disco. You comin, Rain*bow*?"

"Have to ask my mother."

"Well, ask her."

"Can I go to canteen, Kathie?"

"No, you have homework to do."

"Not tonight, Kathie."

"Then you can stay and help me here."

Eljay strolled on out. She gave me what-for. Didn't like him or any of the other boys to drop around, also let me know she didn't go for my friend Beryl.

"That womanish piece switches herself from side to side like sayin look everybody, see what I got."

Eljay was distant for most a week, also loud-mouthed bout my name bein _Rainbow._ I cooled with Beryl cause you can't act chummy and ask someone _not_ to come to your house. Eljay finally broke down, waited for me after school. Said, "Nothin was to laugh bout, I dig the name Rainbow. It suit you cause you so pretty . . . just hit me off my guard, that's all." I had to tell Beryl that my mother didn't like me havin home company. So whenever Kathie cut out I'd go to canteen or wherever and get back fore she knew I was gone. One thing, easy to beat her home cause she knows how to be gone for a long time.

No friends-a mine ever behave like Burke. He can act up. He's a liquor drinker and will turn out when juice get to his head. Other times he could be right nice. Come by bringing fruit, colas or ice cream. He say, "I took the pledge! Burke's on the wagon!" He taught me to play Hearts, Tonk and Draw Poker. We played for Pokeno chips, not money. Good thing cause he won all my chips. He bought Kathie a set of perfume with soap and talcum. But I didn't go for him gettin too close.

Who knows, Leroy might be comin back. One month my father sent *two* checks. But he has a girlfriend in Detroit.

Kathie say, "So much for that Leroy, through is through."

He came back to see us one Christmas, also one Easter. He hug Kathie and kiss her a smack on the neck. She push him away . . . "Okay, lover, don't start nothin and there won't be nothin." He just laugh. He hug me too.

This mornin I tried to explain that Burke to our case-worker. He might right now have my mother somewhere tryin to kill her. Trouble is, Kathie has gone off too many times. There was the night of the fire. Another year she went to go-go up in Boston and was snowed in for two days. Club owner didn't pay her either. Another time she left me with money and went off on a party with her music friends. That weekend the pipes burst in the apartment upstairs. Flooded out! A neighbor took me in but had nothin to do but report Kathie to Social Services. She coulda played cool for a couple-a days. I was placed in the "interim" home. Caseworker thinks my mother is off again havin a ball. All I know is she and Burke left together a week ago and now the eviction notice is up. Wish I could tell Eljay all that's in my heart. I love him but can't yet trust to tell him all. Must be eight girls followin after him. Some lookin fine as movie stars. More than a few also *puttin out.* They bed down with guys . . . not always the same guy. Some takin birth control pills and also got other secret things to do not to get caught. They gettin caught right on. When they do . . . they just live on and tough it out. Some laugh at them. Nobody gets laughed at as much as those, like me, who not puttin out. If ever I do . . . it will be for the one and only *Eljay*. I don't wanta . . . yet.

Goin back to Miss Josephine, I don't really wanta make another return appearance. She be tippin round dainty-like in her too-high heels. Hangin pictures and fixin her apartment to look like a supermarket magazine. She look at the dinner plan and the pictures . . . then got it and gone. Had a steak dinner for her husband's birthday. Warmed the plates in the oven fore she served the broiled sirloin. Gives Harold Lamont the magazine best of everything. One night she made a KEESH for supper . . . a white folks' cheese pie steada real food. Nicest though was the bottle of champagne iced in a bucket. That was for the birthday sirloin supper. She *chill* the glasses in the fridge. She is too much! Heatin plates and chillin glasses. She gave me a taste in a long-stem glass. She say, "Please, Rainbow, don't tell the agency about this. Champagne is alcoholic and you are a minor . . . but I don't want to toast Harold without including you. It's so nice for a toast to be bubbly . . . now, this is our secret . . ."

Shoot, if she knew! Kids round my school sellin grass, pills, angel dust and anything that got a name. I walk on by that crap every day and never worry my mother, Social Services or anybody else. I just don't use and not scared to say . . . "No, thank you." I take care not to upset grown folk bout what's out there. What *can* they do? What *do* they do? Nothin! Outside the Teen Canteen, boys drinkin beer and pints-a wine . . . which they hold in paper bags, be puffin weed at the same time.

Wish I could tell somebody how I feel, bout Kathie

droppin in and out like she do once in a while. That's been the toughest thing. Miss Josie always doin things to uplift *me*. I ain't doin nothin, it's Kathie who drops out. Mayola, our caseworker, say . . . "Josephine Lamont is a fine role model for you." Well, one thing in my favor, I lie to keep the family situation in check. I tell Eljay and my friend Beryl that Miss Josie is my aunt, on my father's side; how the reason I'm back and forth with her is cause my mother be workin outta town. Gotta explain somethin sometime . . . but without puttin all our business in the street. Lotta people will mouth your business to the world if they ever peep your personal secrets. Like when I went to the circus and saw a man walkin the high wire and keepin his balance . . . Ha! Ask me about it. I do it every day.

8. RAINBOW

"You're too young to have so many memories." My
mother said that when I was goin over all the places I've
stayed for "interim." She look sad and didn't wanta hear
bout them. Yes, I have memories and every day I pile
on more. I have more than my friend Beryl or my guy,
Eljay. He never talk bout the past . . . no more than
maybe yesterday or last week. He can't recall what presents he got last Christmas.

"What I care bout back then? This is *now*. My head
is on what's comin up, not what's been."

Kathie and Eljay, two people I dig the most, neither
one like remembering.

Miss Josephine's eyes light up when remembering.
Sometime she will stop and change the subject. When
she turns off her memory you can't push her back on the
case. She will change topics three, four times, just to
throw you off. She goes into that act when discussin her
husband, Mr. Hal. I didn't mean it like to be knockin
him . . . but one day I say . . . "Mr. Lamont sometime
seem too polite. When you go to put on a sweater . . .
he jump up to help you in it, the same when you put

on your coat. I was thinkin maybe you had a sprain arm or something. He also open doors and pull out chairs at the table. I told my mother that if I ever saw a over-polite man . . . it's Mr. Harold Lamont." She look at me real funny . . . then change the subject. Hate to admit, but for some reason, Miss Josie is who I enjoy talking with the most. Would be easy to like her a lot if I wasn't wise to how people can draw you close, then turn you loose.

Tellin things to anybody can be risky. They laugh and put you down bout what you think. I swallow down a lotta words I wanta speak out. Try to force myself to say more to Eljay . . . but I still plan what I say. Want him to admire where I'm comin from. When I'm serious he gets restless, then laugh . . . but nicely. Chucks my chin. "That's cute, you a real fox."

No doubt about it, Miss Josie is best to match thoughts with. Has one fault. She's too humble. So kind she let other people win arguments even when she's right. With Mr. Hal, she lets him win, no matter what. "Well, well, is that right? Harold, I never looked at it in just that way. I see what you mean, dear." Sometime I think she don't even be hearin what he said. He know all about accountin and keepin books for business people . . . but if she didn't wind his watch he'd never make time. He be lookin tall, handsome, neat and clean . . . also a pleasant person. Not grumblin and tellin off women and complainin like some simpleton fellas that come home with Kathie. But no need to think Harold Lamont somehow outshinin the sun, moon and stars. She go on over him like a movie star. If he was to say, "Come, Josephine, let's jump off the Empire State Building," she'd smile and say, "Of course, dear, I would have never

thought of that." She's a ordinary woman livin on a
ordinary block . . . but actin like nothin but happiness
is all around. She the one oughta be name *Rainbow*.
Hard to believe they been married bow-coo years. She
makes a production outta what to buy for his daily dinner
when it's no holiday or birthday. She be pickin through
the vegetables . . . "Oh, I wouldn't want to serve this to
Harold. Let's walk across the way and buy *beefsteak* to-
matoes. Hothouse produce is not for him." She finds the
best of what's out there and serves him only the choice
part-a that . . . and will *apologize*, "Sorry, dear, I
couldn't find a sprig of watercress today."

No way I could be that perfect day in and out without
missin. She's good to me also, a all-around good person
but nowhere near as pretty as my mother. When Kathie's
on the beam there's no one in the world better, none
more fun either. She likes Miss Josie but can put on a
mean imitation of "Old Miss Young," as she calls her.
Throws her head back and smiles. "I do wish Harold and
I could visit Europe, or take in Mardi Gras through the
Caribbean. This year we even missed the cherry blossoms
abloom at Washington, D.C." I fall out the way my
mother say "*a-bloom*" and be wavin one hand like
showin cherry blossoms. But we be likin the lady anyway.
When Kathie show up after bein long gone, Miss Josephine greet her like she's the boss guest we been waitin
for. "Well, what a delightful moment, it's Kathie Jordan.
Do sit down and stay for dinner. I won't take no for an
answer."

Miss Josie is really fine when I need to talk memories.
There's a good teacher at school who makes us go into
stuff that people never used to mention. She have us

talkin bout strange things like death and sayin final fare-well to loved ones. Serious subject. But how bout the loss of a loved one who still livin? When my mother is away it feel like death; but when she's back it's like life again. Was death when Eljay most stopped speakin for a week just cause I'm still holdin out bout goin "all the way." He say, "If you love me you'd be willin to give up somethin. What you savin it for?"

"If I was to get pregnant my mother would kill me."

"Rainey, lotsa things to keep from gettin that way. Talk with Beryl. She pretty smart and been makin out with Buster. Sex is healthy. Ain't nothin bad. It's nor-mal."

"I don't think it's bad. I'm just scared."

"Rainey, let's you and me stop hangin out together. You keep my nerves tore up."

He walked off and it was like "death experience" we discuss in Miss Townes' class. But "dead" is like the end. The dead one didn't mean to leave you on purpose. But when the livin turn their back . . . that's rough. There's been a kinda coolish split with my friend Beryl. I hated to turn my back and give her up . . . but she pushed me to do it.

Beryl is, as far as I'm concerned, the best-lookin girl in ninth grade . . . and we've been in the same class together since bottom of the seventh. Her father is a taxi driver. Her mother works night shift at the General Post Office. Her father works night tour so he can be off same time as when his wife is home. They have a half-interest, with friends, in a frankfurter joint called "The Big Dog Take-Out." Motto is "Don't forget to walk your dog." It's a long counter but no stools for sittin down. Beryl's

mother say, "Lettum bag the crap and keep it movin
. . . so the place won't be a hangout." They put in their
days at "The Big Dog." They don't sleep much but always smilin cause, like Beryl say, "They makin bow-coo
money."

Them bein gone leaves Beryl havin the six-room apartment mostly to herself. Talk bout *fine*. It's a gas. Beryl
likes me cause she say I'm the first one she's met who
can be told a secret and *keep* it. That's for sure. My
mother always say . . . "Every friend got a friend . . .
so keep your mouth shut if you wanta keep your business
off the street." I run my mouth but I know what not to
tell.

Visitin Beryl was a groove. At our place, Kathie doesn't
like me to have company when she's not at home . . .
not too tough bout it when she is home. So Beryl's was
a great place to go. She can have all the company she
want.

Beryl's place is boss. Rose-color rug on the floor, blue
glass mirror all over one livin room wall, white furry
livin room set and black and white draw drapes. Two big
lamps, one on each side-a the couch. One lamp is a
man, the other a woman and each is holdin a lampshade
like it's a umbrella, with beads round the edge. In their
kitchen the fridge makes ice and pops it out automatic,
also got two faucets, one ice water and the other hot for
tea or coffee. The stove oven clean itself and they also
got a microwave for jiffy cookin. The bathroom is pink
tile with black, smoky glass on the wall. They *got* it.

Miss Josie say it sound "tacky." Well, she do things
too quiet. I ask her, "How come everything in your house
is mostly gray and brown?" She say, "I like *muted*

shades." I say, if anybody gonna blow a lotta bread on
furniture, no sense in bein *muted.*

Beryl's closet is fulla clothes. She got a pink joggin
suit with red sequins down one side. Sharpies drop in
the Big Dog and be sellin "hot goods" . . . anything
you can name . . . hi-fi boxes, furs, portable TV, ice
skates, skateboards, everything. Beryl's mother didn't pay
but sixteen dollars for the jog suit. It's a famous brand
that sell for like seventy dollars. I told Kathie maybe we
could buy clothes from the Big Dog. My mother shook
her head. "No, honey, that's stolen goods and I don't
care to wear it. Once I bought me a leather purse 'hot'
but never got any pleasure out of it. What'll I say if
somebody break in here and steal off me? Don't bring in
nothin hot, also stay outta the Big Dog." I did. But went
to Beryl's house at lunchtime cause she was nearer to
school than our house. We had fun. Her fridge is forever
full-a choice cold cuts and like that. Nothin chinchy
bout Beryl. She'd give me what I wanted and throw away
my peanut butter and jelly. Beryl also had spendin
money and used to give me some. Even though her
parents work hard I wondered how come she had three,
four dollars spendin change *every* day.

One day, stead-a goin to her house, Beryl took me by
to see her friend Don. He live round the corner and
older than Miss Josephine. He look like just woke up,
draggin round in his bathrobe and slippers . . . rubbin
the sleep outta his eyes. "Hey there, little jail-bait,
mama!" he holler. "Who's your baby-face friend?" Beryl
help herself to a can-a soda from his fridge and serve it
to me at his *bar.* The bar and also the stool I sat on look
like from out a movin picture bout the tropics. He sat

on the other stool and say, "Ain't you pretty. Lemmie feel you for good luck." He rub my arm. I moved. He laugh and so did Beryl. "Girl," he say. "I ain no trouble, just playin. This ole boy is wore out. All I need to get my jollies is a look and a feel. See here?" He put Beryl's foot up on his knee and ran his hand over her leg. "Just a touch, that's all Don need." When we were leavin he handed Beryl three dollars and gave me one. I said, "No, thank you." He laugh and stamp his foot up and down. "Baby doll, never say *no* to money. Grab it! Snatch it and walk! Cash ain't trash!" Beryl took it. "I'll hold it for her, Don." He was still laughin after he shut and lock the door behind us.

I don't like Don. Couple-a times when she wanted to stop by and "put the beg on him" . . . I wouldn't go. It made a funny feelin between us for a day or so. Finally she drop him outta our plans and we just went to her house or for walks. It was good to have Beryl to talk to bout boys. I never told her bout my "interim" stuff. No way to really talk a problem with a person who never had the same kind . . . not easy, no way.

We were goin to her place for lunch. "Rainey," she say, "when you gonna join the club?"

"What club?"

"Talkin bout you givin some to Eljay."

"Oh, that . . . I don't know."

"I do for Buster. Everybody who turns on is really laughin at how Eljay beggin you and gettin nowhere."

"Everybody don't know my business."

"All I ask is where you comin from? Do you think you better than I am cause I turn on for Buster? You think you too good to give up for a fella you love? Feel like

I'm friends with somebody who lookin down on me."
"I don't think that way, Beryl."
"Other people sayin you do . . . the 'in' girls."
"I don't care what they think. They don't bother with
me noway cause I don't have the latest clothes."
"I'd letcha borrow some-a mine."
"Thanks, but my mother wouldn't dig that."
"Shit, girl . . . you too chicken, scared-a everything."
"Sometimes I am."
"I hear she's a go-go dancer. That's old-timey. Disco
now."
"Who say she's a go-go?"
"No matter, skip it."
I figure it had to be Eljay cause he's the one I told.
Eljay got a mouth that runs off like a dose-a magnesia.
All that talk, talk, talk is what I call "the little *livin
death*" . . . when what the teacher be talkin bout is the
real thing. We were standin outside the supermarket.
Beryl took my hand and say, "Let's buy lunch."
"We have enough. I got my sandwich and you have
food at home."
"Come on Rainey, I always want some of what I don't
have."
It was nice inside the market, air-condition goin and
soft music. We look over the deli section. "Hey," she
say, "you want shrimp?" I say, "No, I like Portuguese
sardines in olive oil."
"Yuk! Shrimp is more my bag."
Lookin at that counter made me remember the second
interim with Miss Josephine and Mr. Hal, how she made
a salad with boneless Portuguese sardines . . . skinless
and boneless, with fresh scallions and homemade dress-
ing . . . yellow candles and white wine. . . .

"You girls get out of this store and never come back."
"Why?" I asked, "We're not doin anything."
The guard grabbed my shoulder and gave a push. "I said get going before I call the cops. I'm trying to give you a break! Out!"
People were gatherin. "We haven't done anything," I said.
Beryl took me by the hand and pulled me toward the door, whisperin, "C'mon, Rainey, let's go, don't make a fuss."
I made a big to-do. "No, why should we be chased?"
She squeezed my hand until the knuckles hurt. Her signal meant "walk." We hurried on out with all eyes followin. The store guard stood on the sidewalk givin us the evil eye.
We didn't speak until enterin her house. "Beryl," I ask, "why did you back down?"
"It's in your coat pocket, Rainey, the sardines. I dropped a can in your pocket."
She opened the can for lunch. I ate some too. Tasted like sadness, not sardines. My "friend" had dropped what she stole into *my* pocket. If I had been searched they would have found it. Would she have confessed that she put it there? I bet not. No way. Remembering my mother's police record . . . and mine, I knew I'd be on my way to a home for delinquent girls; with my mother hauled into court again. I ate sardines with tears on my cheeks.
"Hey, Rainey, what's with you?"
"Nothin much."
Dyin stays too much on my mind. Like in "Death Studies." They say it's hard losin a loved one. But Beryl is still alive, that's not a part of Death Study a-tall. Beryl

is dyin out for me, becomin someone in the past, a memory. No more mirrors and rose carpets . . . no more best friend. She's almost dead inside of me. Like Miss Josie say . . . "I like *muted* better." But I be missin her. Beryl had loaned me her sex book with illustrated positions. I plan to give it back.

Now everybody is talkin bout her cause they say she's pregnant. Her sex book tells about birth control, condoms, pills . . . all sorts of ways to have sex and yet keep from gettin in trouble. But Beryl is pregnant. She's thinkin I stay outta her way just cause she plans to leave school. Wish I could explain how it's really bout Portuguese sardines . . . and that man name Don . . . and not this later happenin . . . which mighta been just a case-a nature shovin her around . . . and like a natural accident.

9. JOSEPHINE

Well, I opened my arms and made her welcome. But thank the Lord—at last there's a moment for myself. "I'm too big to take naps," she said. The girl was so tired she could barely keep her eyes open. "Just lie down and count from two hundred back down to one." She's asleep. A chance to rest my mind. This is not the best day for me to receive an interim child. I could use six weeks to shut out the world. Life sends one emergency after another whenever my mind is operating on last-rinse cycle. I'm trying to avoid thoughts of Harold. Burned a hole in Mrs. Anderson's chiffon stole. Have to match the material, recut, and remake it. I was giving it a light press, my hand stopped moving the iron . . . then smoke. The dial was not set on silk . . . but linen.

I don't know how I got through Mayola doing polite time with us, looking at her watch, longing to leave. Caseworkers put in a certain amount of lingering, as a courtesy. It would look too heartless to dump "the ward" and run. Mayola does her job, and it is not one to envy; collecting abused children or taking them to placement. Some parent or guardian is usually angry with her ar-

rangements, that or resentful. Even the children often
rebel when someone is trying to help. Don't I know?

If Mayola had looked at that watch just one more time
I might have screamed.

Caring for a fourteen-year-old makes me too watchful.
A guardian can guard too much. A guardian is not a
parent or relative. I feel like the villain. I gave her a time
to be in the house. I try too hard to fill her days with
"things to do" . . . homework, reading, helping out with
shopping and dinner. I care and know more about her
than she dreams. I don't think this child notices or knows
anything at all about me. I doubt if she realizes I even
exist. A sound . . . I look up . . . She's standing in the
doorway, still sleepy-eyed.

"I fell asleep?"

"What do you think?"

"I know I did. You want me to do anything?"

"Set the dinner table. Two places."

A cloud in her eyes. "Just for you and Mr. Hal?"

"No, for us. He's out of town."

She now takes some pride in doing a nice table setting.
The first repeat "interim" day is always our difficult one.
We must start all over at trying to be friends. Being a
"repeater" is difficult for "guest" and "temporary guardian." She knows I know it has gone wrong again but
can't unburden herself. We talk about other things and
shy away from painful truth. Sometimes her mother's
name is on my lips and I remember, just in time, to talk
of something else. She must think I'm a slave driver or
else a mighty restless person. I find so many ways to fill
in her visits. She helps take out basting stitches, to shop
the open-air market for greens; goes downtown with me
to select sewing materials, once attended two "women's"

lectures at the Y, also on "Poetry Today." Tomorrow I'll
take her to the Museum of Art. Saturday we'll safari out
to the suburbs, if I've repaired the chiffon damage, so I
can do final fitting for Mrs. Anderson's dress. Two rea-
sons I'm taking her, the first is that it's not right to leave
her alone, the second is . . . I want her to see how
prosperous a Black family can be when they work together. Mrs. Anderson is a smart young matron we might
all do well to emulate . . . if that were possible. She's
well-educated without being tedious about it, also well-
dressed and relaxed in appearance. Barbara Anderson
wears her clothes, they don't wear her. It's a pleasure to
sew for her. She respects my labor. I made her a red silk
dress. She gracefully wore it with a casual air . . . as if
it were a cotton smock, easygoing and so sure of herself.
There is a just-right way some women attain . . . the
right weight, appearance, manner . . . the home environment is comfortable, decorative and well-kept . . .
and the lady of the house looks completely rested and
relaxed through it all. I can't really do it no matter how
I try. I get tired. But I want Rainbow to see it. I wait
until dessert time to inform her about going to my Anderson dress fitting the day after . . . the museum. Rainbow does not glow. She has her own weekend plans.

"Eljay ask me to meet him at Teen Canteen. He
doesn't know I'm now with you. He'll be worryin and
wonderin. Also, I have to check out the apartment every
day. Suppose my mother gets back and doesn't know
where I am?"

"She'll know. Mayola left the note."

"Suppose . . . suppose somethin terrible has happened
to her?"

"Let's not expect that. She's alive and well just as sure

as I'm fifty years old. However, what if something happened and you're over at the canteen?"

She stirs her ice cream while trying to think of another
out. Last time she was here I told her about stirring food
to mush before eating . . . mixing green peas into the
rice until it becomes one common thing. Seems like she
makes baby food out of each meal. Now she's crumbling
the sugar wafer into the ice cream. We couldn't venture
into a first-class restaurant acting like that. A reflection
on the race.

"Miss Josie, if I don't check out our apartment somebody might break in and rob us. Lady next door had her
TV and radio stolen, also a winter coat."

"We'll go check together. Rainbow, you can't be there
all the time, no matter what."

She gives a sigh and a half-smile. "Miss Josie, you
somethin else, you really are."

We have a nice bus trip to the museum by riding
during the off-hours, to miss the crowd. Harold always
advised off-hours. It's costing carfare plus a dollar each
to go in. A man stands behind a turnstile with a sign
. . . Donation—$1.00. The best things in life are no
longer free. We move through long, high-arched marble
hallways, a quiet atmosphere.

"Rainbow, there's a lot more to a museum than things
on exhibit. In this noisy world there are two places where
one may yet go to do some quiet soul-searching. Mu-
seums and public libraries."

"What about churches?"

"The minister keeps talking and when he stops someone is singing or announcing things. However, there are
churches where the doors are open on weekdays. Soon

people will have to go searching for quiet like they used
to hunt wild game."

We roam through the Egyptian Room and study pretty
bracelets and rings made three thousand years ago. Rainbow gazed long at a small, tattered pair of leather slippers. They were once worn by a little Egyptian girl. I
drifted away, returned, she was still there. "Miss Josie,"
she said, "like one time there was a fire and the only
thing I thought to save was my shoes. I'm feelin like
whoever wore those slippers is my little sister."

She meant it. I was touched. "Rainbow, she is related
to you down through the centuries. Time and distance
cannot separate kindred souls."

We share our brown-bag lunch by the outdoor foun-
tain. A warm day but a coolish breeze comes by and tree
leaves whisper. "Nature is showing off," I said, "putting
on airs for our benefit." She smiles. I'm hoping she's
glad we're together and liking the red ribbon I tied on
the lunch bag. Maybe feeling less pain about missing the
canteen party. Of course, I realize that a live boyfriend
is a lot more fun than an Egyptian sister . . . over two
thousand years old. But the friendly mood brought on
by Little Egypt is shaping our thoughts . . . even after
all that time.

"Miss Josie, where's Mr. Hal? Why do you look away
when I mention his name?"

There's an old saying, "Play with a puppy and he'll
lick your mouth," which means "Familiarity breeds con-
tempt." I remind myself that she is only a child. It's
natural for her to express curiosity. I, on the other hand,
am careful about avoiding her home life as a topic of
conversation.

"Hal is down in Atlanta visiting his niece. Her husband is ill. He went to help her manage their real-estate business."

My eyes follow the flight of a flock of pigeons . . . to close the subject. "My, my, see how they fly, Rainbow?"

"No one else can manage their business?"

"They'd rather have a family member. That largest pigeon bullies all the rest. Watch how he struts."

"How long will Mr. Hal be gone?"

"For a while. Never can tell about illness. See, watch how the big pigeon snaps up all the crumbs."

"Will you go down there to be with him?"

"No, there's lots of sewing."

"What about his job? Does he still do accounts for people?"

"Dammit, there is such a thing as taking a leave of absence!"

"Sorry, I didn't mean to bug you."

She takes advantage of my rudeness. "Let's stop by my mother's place and check out that nothing happened." I give in and go four blocks out of my way . . . to get back in her good graces.

We walked up three flights and looked through three drab rooms. The note is still on the dresser where it was left. "Dear Kathie, Rainbow is at Miss Josephine's. There was a rent notice but I got a court stay in hope that you will soon be home. Fondly, Mayola." I wait while she gets her sweater out of the closet, has a drink of water and rearranges her mother's shoes and bathrobe. Our Egyptian sister seems very far away, out of touch with this walk-up apartment.

If Barbara Anderson wasn't such a lovely person there's

no way I'd have kept her as a client after she left the city
for the suburbs. It's a case of I'm having to give more
service than she can pay for. It means giving a whole day
as well as work energy. The phone goes from morning
to night. Her appointment book is the most used item
in the house. She uses twenty-four hours to the hilt.
Never a moment to do nothing-much-in-particular.
Time is never frittered away. She's on benefit committees
to help orphans, the sick and the hungry. Mrs. Anderson
is a constant chairperson. I wish they would hire her to
straighten out the United States government . . . she'd
have it together in no time, without creating ill will.
Well, she is a special look . . . Rainbow should see how
some Blacks are making it . . . to know that all of us
don't have to scuffle and just stay down on the bottom.

Mrs. Anderson does have a houseworker in for three
days a week . . . but juggles the rest on her own. There
are luncheons, Sunday cookouts, overnight guests, midnight swim parties . . . always for a good cause and reason. Her husband has a constant flow of other lawyers
and business acquaintances . . . in and out and out and
in. Makes me tired just to watch the progress of the race;
but I'm proud of her looking like a movie star while
working like a dray horse. If one appointment ends at
two P.M., the next begins at 2:01 . . . and she's level-
headed through every minute. She runs that pretty house
and uplifts her community. Her two children share
"planned time" with their parents . . . and they do
"projects" together. Every evening she changes into some
long, floaty outfit . . . and greets her husband with a
warm smile and a cold drink. Well, I do my best . . .
but she's living ahead of *Vogue* while I'm trying to catch
up with *Family Circle*.

I asked her if I could bring Rainbow for the fitting, also explained a bit of her circumstances. "What a privilege, Josie, a delightful surprise." I knew she'd say that. Nothing is ever too much for Mrs. Anderson. She's slender, good-looking, full of energy . . . and never seems to eat anything but celery sticks and clear bouillon. Well, I can't attain it.

After the fitting, she took over Rainbow. I stayed in the workroom taking in a waistband one size smaller and hand-rolling the hem of her chiffon. Meanwhile, the PTA president dropped by and they had a "pool meeting." Rainbow took a swim. After that . . . she took the child to the Bon Chance Tearoom for a lunch meeting with the Committee for a Clean Environment . . . Chapter Six. They got back just in time to box surprise presents for hospital shut-ins. Poor me, I was barely finished hand-hemming five yards of chiffon. Come to think of it, some people can change the world while I ply this needle in and out of a piece of cloth.

Mrs. Anderson had to drive to the next town so we could catch the express train we missed at her station. She caught it. We managed to climb aboard, with the help of the conductor, just as the train was rolling. Rainbow was impressed.

"That lady can catch an express train."

"Yes, my dear, she's one of us who has managed to get over into middle-class promise-land. She and Attorney Anderson are building interracial understanding, integrating neighborhoods in a positive manner and doing endless good deeds while taking care not to neglect their own. She's a fine, good lady and knows how to juggle

twelve oranges at once. Me, I get worn down making
this trip and turning a five-yard hem."

Rainbow didn't want to leave me out in the cold
. . . feeling inferior. "Miss Josie, you too could do all
those things if you tried."

"Afraid not. I have to leave room to go to a museum
and meet our little Egyptian sister . . . and time to watch
pigeons."

"You don't think she finds time to visit a museum?"

"I'm sure she does. But you can't meet 'Little Egypt'
by calendar appointment. You have to linger and be still
. . . to see if her shoes are ready to speak, understand?"

"You mean she's trying to do too much?"

"She's doing fine, dancing to many fine tunes. I mean
. . . I can't give any more than I'm giving . . . without
dropping in my tracks. I . . . I just can't give a bit more
to Harold . . . or you . . . to anybody!"

"Miss Josie, you mad with me?"

"Of course not."

"You sound mad."

"Oh, don't be so picky."

"Yes, mam."

10. KATHIE

Burke is not to be believed. How can he *love* me and do nothin but make lotta damn-ass trouble? All I hear is . . . "I'm crazy bout you." So busy lovin me till he knocked me almost senseless. Talkin bout I was gettin too chummy "with the damn desk clerk." The man was bout to ring the bell for a hop to come pick up my bag; just for fun I beat him to it and rang the bell myself, okay? How is that chummy?

Burke got me the gig, but soon's we get here it's cancel. I got no contract to back up my case. So, who owes me what? I'm eighty damn miles away from home. What I'm to do? Go to small-claim court and sue over one hundred and seventy-five bucks? Me, I don't wanta go near no kinda court. They go to buttin in my business, call in Social Services . . . next thing they'll sock it to me and Rainbow. This much I know, the next one that hire me to dance . . . they gon pay down somethin in front. These ugly jokers that own "The Everything Goes Club" got the nerve to cancel me out while I'm on the road drivin up here with this fool, Burke.

"Sorry, but we don't have any audience or guests. The

weather is bad and that's against you."

Here I am up in these drafty mountains with a dollar and a quarter to my name. Burke's car got everything wrong with it. He had to put it in the shop. The "resort" owner say all he can do is let us stay in the hotel part at cut rate; then I can work next week when there's three guaranteed bus loads of guests. Gonna *charge* me a rate! That's cold. Expect this from Whitey, but my own is pullin this deal. "Big Jim," the owner, is black as midnight on Halloween and doin me in without blinkin. All trick and no treat. Burke smile at him, shake hands and say we'll take the cut rate . . . which they can *deduct* outta my next weekend pay. Feel like I'm bein had. I'm owin everybody but nobody owin me. I got to deliver a show, pay rent . . . and also shack up for four days with Burke. It's pourin, but damn if it's rain.

I try not to take it out on Burke. He did drive me here. Used his car when it should not be on the road. His insurance ran out. Now he's in hock for repairs. It's a disgustin fix, but he did not have to buy two fifths of hundred-proof bourbon. "Damn," he say. "I may's well relax and enjoy the motel. I can't make it back to my slave job . . . and they sure gonna kick my butt outta steam-pressin bathrobes. Five million niggas waitin on line to take over my minimum wage."

Talk bout tough figurin. If I wanta go home it mean callin someone *collect* . . . to try and borrow. Burke don't want me to leave him and the broke-down car out here in the mountains. One thing buggin me is how poor Rainbow gonna do. We got one rent notice as a warnin. Our landlord is dispossess crazy. He'll tack up the paper while you on the way over to pay. That Big

Jim say we can eat on *"credick"* while waitin for my next weekend gig. He say I can dance Thursday, Friday, Saturday and a Sunday early-bird show.Credit food will wipe out all my profit. Burke tryin to save the day by spendin the rest-a his bread on pizza and hamburgers . . . to go. I'm tryin to ride with the tide. Nothin else to do. I had me a plan to use this gig to pay rent and food till the A.D.C. check. Well, that was then.

This motel room is not the worst. Full-length draw drapes. Never had any at home. I pull them open and pull them shut, they sharp. Two double beds in the room, more bed space than I ever had. Lamps kinda nice. Enter the room, click the wall switch and the lamps light up. White telephone on the bedside table. Blue wall-to-wall carpet on the floor. In the bathroom a gold-streaked sorta marble sink. Got glasses wrapped in clear plastic, a ice bucket. Stacks of thick towels . . . hand, bath and face. A color TV in the room, can turn it round to watch while in bed. When I stop thinkin bout Rainbow . . . I have a nice time with Burke. We put soft jazz on the radio, also have ice cubes from the machine down the hall . . . to go with our bourbon . . . also got us a order of Kentucky chicken and fries. Nice of him to buy the order on the way back from the cheatin garage.

Burke knows how to make love, kisses nicely. I could really have a good time . . . except for worryin bout Rainbow. No way to forget her with rent due and me stranded . . . pleasant as a strand might be. I say a silent prayer while Burke is again sayin how much he loves me. All of a sudden the answer to my prayer goes blinkin through my head like an electric sign.

"Burke, I'm gonna call Rainbow's father. He'll send the rent. Leroy is sometime cool like that."

He jump up and start walkin the floor. "Leroy? If he got rent money how come he ain't sent it in the first place?"

"I gotta call for Rainbow's sake. I don't want her sittin on the street. They'll bring me up on charges. Burke, don't act the fool."

He's pourin himself more hundred-proof while gettin mad and loud. "Leroy is out of it! Call the Social Service. You tryin to get back in with him?"

"No, honey, but let him take on some of the weight. Leave Social Service alone. Start with them and they don't know how to stop. He'll do for *her*, not me. Let's let Leroy come through and telegram a check direct to the house."

"Call Rainbow! If all is okay, you don't have to talk to anybody a-tall! She can wait till we get back!"

"I called, there was no answer!"

"Call again!"

"If I get her and *then* call Leroy . . . that'll be two long-distance calls. I'm long-distancin on money I haven't even made yet, right?"

"Ain't I spendin mine?"

"Burke, please don't drink no more till this is settle."

"Okay, call the no-good mother, if you must."

I call Leroy collect at his girlfriend's. She answers. I explain how the long-distance operator gave her number. She accept the call. She's a lady. She say . . . "He'll call Rainbow for you. Ain't one thing it's another, huh? He just stepped out to cash his check. If there's any trouble bout cashin it, I'll draw it out my savins. Like I tell him all the time . . . we gotta help one another these days. We'll take care of it. Don't you worry."

Now that's what I call a *sister*. I didn't tell her how

he was suppose to call two weeks ago . . . but goofed.
Burke is now feelin better. He's pleased Leroy was not
at home, also glad he got a girlfriend. But still mumblin
how Leroy better not show up while he's around.

"Burke, Leroy is way out in Detroit. I haven't seen
him for years."

"But soon as anything happen you gotta call. Suppose
the nigga was dead . . . could you call?"

"Guess not."

"Well, make like he's dead."

"I'm goin over and ask Big Jim advance me some
cash."

"Now you gon grin up to him. Runnin to other cats
is a way-a puttin me down. I don't like it!"

"Your cash is most gone by now."

"So what? Tough it out!"

I try to enjoy the room. There's a machine that vibrates
the bed when you put two quarters in it, shakes for fifteen
minutes. Bathroom has a sun lamp in the ceiling.

"Baby, ain't you black enough?"

"Burke, I gotta do something."

"My company all that bad?"

"No, but you too jealous. You didn't have to hit me
in the elevator bout that desk clerk."

"Didn't hurt you."

"Hittin is hittin. I don't like it."

"Who you callin now?"

"Rainbow. Gotta see if she's okay and explain. No
answer. I'll keep tryin after while."

"You serious bout us or not? First it's Leroy, now it's
Rainbow. Don't play with me. You don't be worryin over
me that way."

"I'm goin for a walk, get some fresh air."

I put on my skirt and sweater while he's pourin another bourbon. I comb my hair and do a dab-a lipstick.

"It's too cold to go out, Kathie."

"I need air, time to think."

"You goin to Big Jim for advance money! I say you not to go!"

"See you in half a hour."

I'm bout to unlock the door. He grabs my arm and almost pulls it out the socket. Sends me sprawlin cross the bed.

"Bitch, don't turn your back on me!"

"Please, Burke, don't start a riot. Take a nap. Sleep it off, you'll feel better."

I still wanta go out but he's gettin madder. "Told you not to go! No woman's gonna play me for a sucker!" Someone in the next room raps on the wall.

"Okay, Burke, I'm stayin here. You are actin ignorant. Please be quiet."

I'm scared to let him raise too much noise. Got no money, in a strange place. I don't need any police trouble. Don't need another round of probation for no reason a-tall. Me, I'm not makin a sound . . . not if he tears my head off. I'm gon listen to this television and keep my cool. Man lookin like a Supreme Court judge is doin a simple-ass commercial . . . ". . . A complete set of the classics with gold-embossed leather-like bindings . . . extended payments . . . interest free . . . money back if not completely delighted . . ." Been a hell of a long time since I been *completely delighted* bout anything. Burke calms down and takes me in his arms.

"Kathie, baby, I act up cause you don't love me much

as I love you. Please don't go out . . . no tellin what I
might do. How come you don't love me much as you
be lovin everybody else?"

We stay in the room for three days. Every time he
falls asleep I call Rainbow . . . there's no answer. That
square, Josephine, doesn't answer either. Everybody's ass
is out in the street except mine. No matter how hard I
try to do the right thing . . . I always mess up. I *can't*
love Burke as much as he loves me . . . maybe can't love
anybody else either. Not a man in this world is takin
care-a me . . . except this clown, Burke. He wakes up
and smilin at me like nothin ever happen.

"Kathie, darlin, want another bourbon?"

"Okay, sweetie. Thank you, Burke. Just a small one
. . . sugar pie."

11. RAINBOW

Why should Miss Josie keep the only key to my apartment? Got the nerve to hang it on a nail inside the door of her dish closet. Hold up one finger and made a rule that I'm not to touch it. I told Eljay. He warn me not to let her win the battle with her jive-humble way. "Rainey, when she split the scene for a hour or two . . . you take your key back. Hang another one in its place. Wear your key round your neck, drop down inside-a your dress. That way she can't steal it back. After all, can you snatch her property? Can you hold up your finger and tell her how things gonna be?" Well, I'll take it when I'm good and ready. Not gonna hang any fake substitute either. Eljay gave me a substitute one but . . . I don't feel like playin games about what's mine.

Nobody would ever have to sneak and do anything if some people didn't make it necessary. They hem you in corners, then demand answers. Miss Paloma stays on me bout bringin my mother to school to talk bout math, also wants her *written* consent for me to take Sex Education with Miss Townes. Kathie already sign for regular Phys. Ed. in the first place, okay? She won't sign for SEX . . . and I damn sure won't explain how my mother *can't*

show cause I don't know where she is. When the last
bell is in I try to file out in the middle of the group. Miss
Paloma is wearin those bottle-bottom glasses like people
who have poor eyesight. She can see 20/20.

"Rainbow, I want to talk to you."

I reminded her yesterday how she used to call me
Rainey for "Laraine." "No," she say . . . "No more. You
were registered as Rainbow Jordan. If it's an error, your
mother can bring in your birth certificate and we'll make
the correction." Her whole aim in life is to track down
small lies that not hurtin anybody. She also know how
to use her so-call "poor vision" to see *everything* . . .
like when I'm trying to slip out and go home in peace.

"Rainbow, I want to talk to you."

"Yes, mam."

"It's 'Yes, Miss Paloma.' "

"Yes, Miss Paloma."

She drop her voice and let me in on the secret. "This
is my final request. You have your mother come to
school."

"She had to go out of town."

"That's understandable. Where is she?"

Every word I know flew away. She was lookin at me,
I'm lookin back. I'm not gonna hand over my soul secrets, or my mother's either. Paloma is white and I do
not need her walkin round feelin sorry for me or havin
me in for their "group discussion" with "staff." I don't
need a whole *group* to zoom in on me as target number
one. She got a Black teacher friend down the hall . . .
and here she come now. Miss Townes is in charge of
Phys. Ed., Sex Ed. and Death Study. Paloma surely
hipped her to show up after class. They actin extra cas-

ual, like it's not a setup.

"Miss Townes, I was just telling Rainbow that she has until next Tuesday to bring her mother to discuss a few problems."

Townes agrees and reminds me that she is only to teach SEX with "parental" consent. I've had two classes by sayin how I forgot to ask for a note. Next time I said I had lost the note. Miss Townes got big, brown innocent eyes and act like every piece-a information is new.

"Oh, I'm sure she will ask her mother to send a note, won't you, dear?"

"Yes, Miss Townes."

They exchange looks with each other like "We gettin somewhere now."

I look up at the ceilin like I'm not noticin their sly ways. My mother is prettier than they are. They could be dressed for a New Year Formal and Kathie would outdo them just wearin her "Honey Buns." After Townes cut out . . . Paloma really turns the knife. "If Mrs. Jordan is not here by next Tuesday, we will have to take another step." Her eyes move in on me like the next step might be the gas chamber or the electric chair. I'm feelin bad but she can't stop her mouth.

"Maybe you have boys on your mind too much."

The cat's out the bag. She hittin below the belt cause Eljay passed me a note . . . *weeks* ago. I was mindin my business and writin a current-events paper on "Trouble in Iran." He wrote the note and handed it to Beryl. She passed it on to me. Miss Paloma's poor eyesight followed every move.

"Rainbow, bring that note to me."

I was dyin. Didn't know what might be *in* the note.

I opened it and read. "I go for you, Rainey, gonna get you in my arms one these days. Bow-coo love . . . Eljay."

"Rainbow, bring that note to me."

If I did I'd never been able to look another soul in the eye. I wondered what she'd do if I handed it over. Read it out loud? Show it to Miss Townes? Might send Eljay to the principal. Send us both? She might show it to my mother if anybody ever get hold of her. Okay, so I hadn't asked him to send me a note and it's *his* note. I folded it, went over to his desk, and handed it back to him.

Paloma turned pink. "Eljay, you bring me that note."

He sat there and tore it into tiny bits and pieces, and tinier yet . . . then walked up and dropped it all on her desk. Would take her years to put that jigsaw together. Class went to laughin and fallin out. Paloma never forgave that. She might forget his part cause they all say "boys will be boys." They not ready for "girls will be girls."

Eljay say, "Okay, I handed it over like you ask." Two rough boys in the back-a the room stood up and clap their hands. "That's right on!" Her eyes stayed dead on me. She was hot cause I had return the note to Eljay . . . scorin a home run for me. I let the *responsible* parties have the *confrontation*. I haven't been through Social Services for nothin. Another thing draggin me is how Miss Josie be takin up for teachers, just cause she once had a perfect teacher name Miss Line. I do believe that experience left her with what's call a teacher-fixation or phobia. Miss Josie is a stone admirer of educators. "More of them are for than against you, Rainbow, they want you to learn and prosper."

All those times when I left Miss Josie and go back home with Kathie . . . I remembered to return now and then to see her like she had ask me to do. She always say, "Don't forget me, Rainbow. Come by some Saturday and give me a hand with sewing." She was teachin me more than I was helpin, also gave me some money. Kathie say, "You go. It's a good idea to learn a trade and become maybe like a dressmaker. You sure couldn't have a better teacher, honey." When I visit Miss Josie . . . Kathie feel free to go out and have a ball with her friends, without worryin if the house is gonna cave in on me while she be gone.

Miss Josie showed me how to adjust a paper pattern before cuttin into your material . . . the garment will fit. She taught me how to press each seam open, so the garment will not look tacky. Also how to hand-hem loosely slack, then press so the hem will not look like factory made. I like sewin. One Saturday we had a big batch-a work. I basted and pressed for her. "Isn't Mr. Hal off on Saturday?" I ask.

"He had extra tax reports and accounting for some clients."

I like the way she and Mr. Hal have "clients" and not "customers." If I ever go in business I will have "clients." That's classy.

All of a sudden he popped in the door. "Hey, Miss Rainbow, how are you today?"

"Fine, Mr. Hal. You finish your taxes and accounting?"

He look puzzled, then said, "Er . . . er . . . well, sure thing."

Miss Josie took him in the livin room and they was

whisperin so I could not hear. She sound angry. They
come back and she say, "We're going out to discuss
. . . to er . . . er see about some business. Do you care
to stay for dinner this evening?"

He say, "We'll see you home. The neighborhood is
changing."

"Changin in what way?" I ask.

He smile in his kindly way. "Just more crowded and
a little rougher than it used to be."

I remember finishin the seams, pullin bastin stitches
and pickin pins off the floor. I also picked loose threads
from the "garments." Miss Josie sews so well she no
longer works on "dresses" . . . only "garments." A garment is better. I set the table the way she likes, with
napkins in water goblets. Gettin so till I like goblets,
cloth napkins and candles lit for dinner. Last A.D.C.
check I bought two goblets and a candle for Kathie and
me, also two navy-blue bandanna kerchiefs to be napkins. Tears came to Kathie's eyes and she say . . . "Keep
goin to Miss Josie. She kinda square but don't give up
on her. Give everybody a chance."

Now I open Josie's front window to look out on the
street, to see how the neighborhood changin. First
change was Eljay on the other side of the street with
Buster and Beryl. I was duckin back in the window and
bumped my head . . .

"Hey, Rainey! Rainey!"

They all lookin up. Eljay glad, "Say . . . Rainey, what
you doin up there?"

"You know this my aunt's house. I . . . I'm visitin."

They come strollin cross the street and into the downstairs. Nobody ask them. Next thing they knockin on the

door and walk on in. Eljay had a jug-a apple wine and
they want glasses. I got paper cups from the kitchen. I
wasn't gonna raid the china cabinet. Told them . . .
"Don't get comfortable. Better drink fast cause my Aunt
Josie don't allow alcohol for the young."

"Who she like it for?" Eljay ask. "For old people?"

Buster cracked up and went to gettin out ice cubes.
Tasted Miss Josie's crabmeat salad.

"Don't touch her dinner," I say. Buster just come out
the funky street and dippin his finger in her glass bowl.

I gave in and took a taste-a the apple wine so's not to
look standoffish and like tryin to be better than my company. Beryl turned on Eljay's Deluxe Eight Band World
Wide Short Wave Box. Box got separate bass and treble
controls. Talk bout some sound. Outta sight. They all
goin to the canteen. Would be the day I had promise
Josephine to hang inside till she and Mr. Hal return.

We fool around and dance little bit and like that. I
never let Buster go back in that fridge again . . . but I
did serve them her crackers and cheese. Gonna buy some
more with my sewin pay. One thing, Eljay will *try* to
respect other people's house. Buster is the one took out
weed and lit up. I say, "Don't do that! The smell be here
and make trouble." Eljay made him put it out. Me, I
don't smoke nothin. I ask them to *go* after they finish
the wine. I didn't drink but a swallow and neither did
Beryl. Buster was the one washin it down like water.
Eljay sip, Buster gulped. He paid a old wino a quarter
to buy the bottle for them. They do anything to make
a quick quarter so they can gather enough to buy they
own bottle. That shouldn't be, but it's the way it is.

In no time a-tall Buster lights up again.

Beryl say, "Why can't you do like Eljay and be cool."

Then Eljay got in it and say . . . "Her aunt don't go for that."

"Fuck her aunt! This shit's mine!"

"Come on, Bus," Eljay say. "Out, time to go!"

"Man, let loose my clothes!"

He pushed Eljay. They both fell against the table and one of the dinner goblets smash to the floor. Miss Josie come walkin in just at the wrong minute; before I could sweep up glass or air the smell out. I almost died. Glad Mr. Hal not with her. She lookin pale as a Easter lily. Eljay shove Buster out in the hall and Beryl follow . . . they ran down the steps. Must have been five minutes fore she spoke to me . . . seem like five.

We both cleanin up, airin out and no talk. I was scared on two counts . . . she might report me to Kathie or Mayola . . . or both. Also shamed of myself and my company. We sure look like the ones who changin the neighborhood. I was sorry to my heart. Scared she might never speak to me again.

"Miss Josie," I say, "I apologize. It's all my fault. Please don't report me."

"I won't. But you are never to have anyone in my home when I am not here, even then you must *first* have my consent."

"Yes, I promise. I'm sorry we ate your crackers and cheese. Please take it outta my pay and buy yourself some more. Pay back is the best I can do."

She blew her cool. "Girl, it is not at all about crackers and cheese. It's about the *bums* you like. That nasty-mouthed boy lighting up the air with his language. He's louder than the music! And that good-for-nothing *Eljay!*

You draw bad company! Now you got one more . . .
Buster! A criminal face if I ever saw one. Such as it is,
my home is my *castle*. I don't owe my heart to you, your
mother, Mayola, Social Services, the community . . .
or *HAROLD!*" She was screamin and pickin up broken
glass till she cut her pinky finger and went to cryin.
"Keep that element out, out, out! I know your parents
don't treat you right, your fathers are not interested and
white folks hate the sight of all of us from slavery up to
now. I *understand* what makes some of us do what we
do . . . but I don't *appreciate* it. Kids out here snatching
purses and beating women and . . . girl, don't bring another lost soul within eyesight! Respect this home or *else!*
If you want to be nothing . . . be it! You're not to drag
me down! I'm not taking another double-damn thing off
you or *Harold Lamont!!*"

They know it all, even Kathie. If I ever had behave
like that Burke they'd put me in reform school. Okay,
so I'm suppose to have *nobody?* There's a girl in school
name Janine, one name Theresa, and there's also Olay-
inka, all of em tryin to get Eljay for themselves. Some
girls try to steal a fella from other girls. Just tryin to show
off and be mean. They like to put you down and try to
make you feel like less than nothin.
Miss Townes held a "consciousness raisin" session for
girls . . . *feminists*. My conscious was raised fore I even
walk in the door. All got to talkin how boys treat girls
. . . but it stop right there. One thing I know, *females*
can be extra mean and critical to each other. They need
to break it on down and deal with that up front, before
takin up males . . . and all that "awareness" shit. An-

other thing, if boys be so damn bad, didn't a woman
mostly raise em in the first place? I'm hearin female
conversation from Kathie, Mayola, Miss Josephine and
my teachers . . . and how bout Beryl and the rest? Like
English Composition say . . . "Et al." Females be clawin
the hell outta one another . . . hurtin each other bout
their hair style, bout havin only one boyfriend or *none*
boyfriend. Girls hate each other for bein too pretty or
too homely, for bein too neat or too sloppy . . . or too
loose or else uptight. But be callin each other "sister."
Some in my school usin "sister" like just another word
for *nigga*. They say . . . "the sister walked in lookin all
wrong" . . . that's meanin your hair style or clothes or
who you with or not with. Soon as one pop look come
in the other is out, so what's the dif? I look how I look,
that's all. You're you, I'm me.

I'm gonna soon have enough of my own money save
so a hairstylist can do me up with beads and braids . . .
big wooden bangers that go clack when I turn my head
. . . then all the so-call brothers and sisters who put
people down . . . they can kiss my natural ass. I'll be
lookin so sexy and fine. Eljay gonna be more than glad
to be on my side when mother, guardian and Social
Service have to move out my way and make room for
progress.

12. RAINBOW

I walk with my head higher now. Some clouds do have a silver linin. Mayola came by after her workday was over, which was nice of her. She had a Leroy money order from our mailbox. The court will hold it for the landlord to collect . . . when Kathie gets back to sign her signature. Another proud thing. Kathie call me at Miss Josie and *explain*. "Honey, I am stranded in the wilderness with my gig called off. I been worried to death when I call home and gettin no answer. I finally got hold-a Mayola." Me, I know she tellin the truth. Like I say to Josie, "People *can't* hear from other people if they gonna be out all the time." Who can reach anybody at the museum or while they at a Clean Environment luncheon?

When Kathie did get to do her act, the next weekend, clients and management like her and holding her over for *two more* weeks. One thing, I'm glad she's a celebrity . . . but wish she was back home. I miss her. Other people no way the same as your own. Sometime Miss Josephine express what I call "hostility." Things goin fine

with us right now, but she is not my family. Soon I'll go
home, so why must she give a talk on language.

"Rainbow, none of us need to use foul words or slangy
talk. I would not be surprised if many women aren't
turned away from sex because the words commonly used
to define the sexual act are usually the vilest kind of
insult to women. Government officials and high-up busi-
nessmen say 'I was screwed' when they mean they were
cheated. They say 'I effed up' whenever they make a
terrible mistake. They call each other mother-effers. The
everyday language tells every woman she's the loser in
the sexual act."

But she did sign a consent slip for Sex Ed. class. Then
add a note to it. "I am now Rainbow's guardian during
the temporary absence of her legal parent." That consent
is still in my purse. Note puts teacher smack-dab in my
personal business. I had ask her to sign "Katherine Jordan" . . . but she would not, sayin it's like forgery. To
me "forgery" would be if somebody sign a false name so
they could cash a check to steal money. In this case she'd
be signin as a positive act.

Adults always tryin to level with each other and come
out honorable-lookin. They don't care what *we* think.
Credit where credit is due. Miss Josie is all for me takin
Sex Education. Kathie was the surprise. Back when I
first mention it she threw the consent slip on the kitchen
table and say, "Kids know enough devilment. They do
better to teach prayer. Little prayer in school might do
you good."

She don't pray, not even meditate like Miss Josie. If
she do be prayin I never saw it. She make *me* go to
Sunday School but she don't hit church except for maybe

Easter . . . that's if we got new outfits. Kathie say, "Can't walk in lookin bad or they'll eyeball you. Also can't wear any my old short dresses or jeans." One time we went to church on Mother's Day. Was nice. I wore a red carnation cause my mother is livin, Kathie wore a white cause hers is dead. Preacher preached bout respect and love for motherhood. A lady sang a song call Mother. The song was explainin how mother is growin old . . . Kathie's not growin old, never will, just prettier and younger. Her astrology sign is Scorpio, mine is Libra the scales. Libra is suppose to know how to balance matters. Wish I did. Leroy is Taurus the bull, they stubborn. Miss Josie is under the sign of Gemini—the twins. She say, "I don't believe in that nonsense. You mean to tell me there are only twelve kinds of people in the world? There must be a thousand different kinds of rascals just on this one block. Act so constantly outrageous they must be under one sign . . . Satan, sign of the devil." She is a true Gemini, with two sides to her character . . . one "float like a butterfly," the other "sting like a bee" . . . like Muhammad Ali say.

Miss Josie is busy goin out on calls to make garment alterations. But won't leave me in the house alone. Sends me to visit her Quaker friend, Miss Rachel. That shows lack of faith. I promised not to have any more company in her house, I mean that. But I dig visitin Miss Rachel. Help me to forget needin Kathie and not bein able to be with Eljay. The Quaker apartment got nice souvenirs from all over the world. She's been to India, Mexico, lotsa places. Got pen-pals writin from foreign countries. They send each other picture postcards and gift "remembrances." She has a rug on her wall like it's a

picture, Oriental rug. Has a fat Russian doll made out
of wood. You open it. Inside is another doll, inside that
is another and another until you get down to the last,
which is tiny . . . all dolls wooden and exactly the same.
She has a German beer stein, keeps peppermint candies
in it. She does not drink alcohol and is mostly vegetarian
except for fish and chicken. I asked her, "Miss Rachel,
are Quakers vegetarian?"

"No, that's personal choice, but we don't believe
smoking, or drinking alcoholic beverages serve any good
purpose in life."

Made me wonder if Miss Josephine told her about the
wine and pot party that happen by accident cause-a
Buster. She might be signifyin.

Miss Rachel is seventy-eight years old. That is old, but
she call herself *elderly*. Like one time Miss Josie was
boastin bout herself bein fifty. I say, just to be talkin,
"Like wow! That's a half a century." She look so hurt.
She say she middle age. You middle age at fifty if you
expect to get to a *hundred*, okay? Quakers do good things
to help the poor. They also helped to free slaves. Some
of them were punished for that. When white people
move away from this "changin neighborhood" . . . Miss
Rachel stay right on. She say, "Whites create changing
communities. One different family arrives and we move
away. If all stay put we'd have a lovely community with
a nice variety of neighbors."

"Why do they move, Miss Rachel?"

"Vanity mostly. We don't want our friends to look
down on us for living in a 'mixed' community."

"Do you think the law can do anything about mixin
neighborhoods nicely?"

"I don't know, Rainbow. The law works when it comes

to making us pay income tax . . . but on racial matters
so many claim we can't legislate change. It must come
about through free will. No taxes would ever be paid if
we waited on free-will offerings."
"No taxes except from a few honest folk, like you."
"Early in life I made it my 'concern' to work for better
racial understanding. That is what Quaker young ladies
had instead of a 'career' . . . we had 'a concern.' I did
not believe God made any errors when he created varied
images of himself. We are all made in the image of
God."
"That's heavy."
"A hymn says . . . We'll understand it better by and
by."
"Miss Rachel, your church is way downtown. Don't
you miss bein close to your white friends?"
"We don't have churches, we have Meeting Houses.
There are a few Black 'Friends' in this area . . . Quakers
. . . but . . . I stay here mainly because the rent is more
reasonable than elsewhere. Also . . . my faith tells me
to keep the faith and stand my ground."
"Yeah, but sometime it pay to move on when cruddy
boys snatch your purse and hurt you."
"Black women are going through the same thing. Why
don't they move?"
"They don't have many places to go, Miss Rachel."
"You found the answer."
"Too many good people be force to live round these
criminals. My mother say that bein poor can keep your
head and handbag in trouble. But mostly she go on tryin
to be good anyway."
"I'm glad."
"Miss Josie say . . . 'Be good sweet maid and let who

will be clever' . . . that's her most favorite poem. Me,
I like Black poets. You ever read any?"

Miss Rachel reads a lot. Enjoys Paul Laurence Dunbar. "I like him too," I say, "but lotsa time I get tired-a
hearin dialect . . . dialect is his main thing."

"Well, those who don't like dialect should not speak
it. We can't fill the air with sound and ask a poet not to
hear. On the other hand, everyday speech of everyday
persons . . . very often becomes the song of many writers
. . . Sean O'Casey, Dunbar, Sholem Aleichem, Coun-
tee Cullen, Langston Hughes, Isaac Peretz."

She gave me a book-a short stories by Peretz, who is
a Jew. We soon gonna have "free choice" book report.
I'm gonna knock Paloma on her ass and leave her with
her mouth wide open. She will not expect me to know
about Peretz. I wish there was "free choice" more often.
I would like to write "A *Study of Parents and Teachers
by the Child.*" Plenty of books on "Child Study." Trouble is, when children get to be adult for a good long time
. . . they forget what it was to be young, then they write
some book. Grown people with bad memories like to
write about children. They be "studyin" kids but got no
feelin left bout what kid-hood was like. All they remember is the good things and never how children can be
worried to death.

Same for race. I told Miss Rachel how there's plenty
books on studyin African, Afro-American, Indian, South
Sea Island and like that. No study bout how we seein
whites behave. Right is right and wrong is a damn drag.

One these bad, BLACK dudes that brute-out just to
jump the helpless . . . snatch Miss Rachel's purse. Hurt
her wrist too. It made me almost mad as it did Miss
Josephine. Look like decent people always catchin it

harder than the rotten. My good deed has been to go shoppin with this Quaker, to help deposit her Social Security check . . . or draw money, however the case may be. Miss Josie goes with her when she can, other times it's me. Miss Rachel say, "I'll really have to *center down* to get over that boy attacking me." Center down . . . meditate thoughts *inward* . . . Quakers turn the problem over to "the silence" . . . Time pass and then a "answer" come to them. They might feel moved to tell others what thoughts came. They don't have a preacher . . . Miss Rachel say each person is a minister. Miss Rachel explain it clear.

If I was to center down on anything, right now, it would be to wonder how Miss Josephine found Beryl's book . . . "Ninety Sex Positions—Illustrated with live models." I had it for months and had only flipped through the pages. Say she found it while cleanin my room. Does anybody clean inside another person's suitcase? No privacy. I meant to return that book. Nothin but people twistin themselves into pretzels to make love. I sure wouldn't want any of those lady models to be my mother. Someday, if I ever have a child, it would be awful for her to open that book and say . . . "Hey, ain't that Grandma?"

One picture was name "The missionary position." Didn't make me think-a missionaries. Miss Josie beg me please not to read trash. Look like she wanta cry. Sex makes parents, teachers and "interim guardians" very sad.

Back to Miss Rachel . . . she like readin my thoughts. She smile sad-like and say, "Josephine tells me they are teaching sex education at your school."

"Yes, mam, you think that's okay?"

"These days people go on like sex was invented last
week. But I guess it's best to study truth."

Miss Rachel starts carin for window plants while discussin sex. She has boards across the windows, like
shelves, for plants needin sunlight. Some in jars of water.
She got a way-a snappin bits off old plants so she can
start new ones. She's now fixin plants so's not to look
directly at me while talkin sex. Josie, Rachel, Kathie
. . . they look away to talk sex. They seem upset but try
to come over cool.

"Miss Rachel, can Sex Study ruin people's morals?"

"Anything is discussable by an intelligent mind. De-
pends on how it's done."

"In class . . . I drew a copy of . . . of a woman's
vagina and a man's penis. Boys cracked up laughin and
actin simple. One said . . . 'Mine don't look that way!' "

"He was probably embarrassed. We're ashamed of our
bodies and their functions. Our nakedness has lost in-
nocence. Shame is what makes 'dirty jokes' funny.
Shame makes lewdness profitable. Rainbow, I hope you
have a good teacher for Sex Education class. She will
face many difficulties."

"Miss Rachel, seem like it's difficult to think out anything."

"Our heads and hearts have to stay in training for it,
like athletes preparing for the Olympics."

I'm glad to do a good deed for her. The deed got even
better. I did not take two dollars she tried to give me.
Not that I can't use two more to save for my beaded hair-
do . . . but it's a drag to think of every move in dollars
and cents. Money stays too much on my mind. I do
need it . . . high bus fare, lunch cost and like that.
Sometime somebody ask me to a party way cross town

and I say, "Sorry, got a date." Big lie. Got no money for
carfare to go or get back. Somethin bout me that hates
to tell. Nobody like to say they broke. Sound like you
unimportant. Eljay wave his hand so grand and say
. . . "Got somethin else goin this Friday." That mean
he's outta bread. Still and all, money shouldn't be a
twenty-four-hour to-do. People talkin checks, rent money,
utility bill and *endless* with it. There's more serious
things.

"Miss Rachel, what you think bout death?"

"I wouldn't miss it for the world."

"You makin a joke. I mean for real."

"Rainbow, all the best people are doing it . . . the
wealthy, the fashionable, and even heads of govern-
ments. Seems to be the 'IN' thing."

For a Quaker she sure know how to make you laugh.
One day she took down her hair and comb it out . . .
white hair, a yard long. She winds it back up tight and
put gray hairpins to hold it. When she finish look like
it's not so long.

"Miss Rachel, when I save up some bread . . . some
money . . . I'm gonna have the hairdresser braid my hair
with golden beads . . . clackers and bangers on the end."

"Clackers? Bangers?"

"Big beads on the end-a each braid, also seashells.
When I shake my head they'll bang and clack. That's a
African style."

"It's expensive?"

"Yes, mam . . . but it lasts for weeks. You can wash
your hair and not even undo it . . . just stand under the
shower beads and all. Yours would be all the way down
to your waist."

"Bet I'd make a 'joyful noise unto the Lord' as I'd go

banging and clacking my way to Quarterly Meeting."
Miss Rachel know how to make me laugh.

Josephine Lamont is not herself. I wish Mr. Hal would
come home. She lookin downhearted. It ain't my fault.
Some friend-a hers died and I went with her to the
"viewin." It was the day before service when people can
go for an advance look at the corpse laid out in pretty
clothes. I'm not scared of the dead cause-a my studies.
Kathie is, she does not go to "view." She say, "Gives me
the shivers." We viewed Josie's friend, then looked in
other little rooms and stared down at different corpses.
One man was really a sharp cat with a blue flower in his
lapel, not lookin like he'd ever been sick. She stood there
lookin at him for the longest kinda time. I say, "A shame
such a handsome man has passed." She say "He didn't
'pass' . . . he died. At last his wife *knows* where to find
him." That's some *cold* talk.
    Tell you bout the sign of Gemini. Two persons in
one. Bad-mouthin the *departed*. Good and sweet as she
can be, but can turn into a stone witch without warnin.
She went through that place and viewed every corpse
that was laid out. Was lookin too *satisfied* over the dead
men.
    I tried to sound sociable. "They all look nice, don't
you think?"
    "No. When I go, just ship me to the crematorium,
turn the leftovers into ashes . . . then blow Josephine
away with the wind."
    "You don't wanta be viewed first?"
    "No. I don't want any two-faced, double-dealing, low-

down rascals to be lookin down on me when I'm helpless and can't look back."

Hey, wow! Mamma mia! Gemini must be outta balance with the moon.

There's this nosy lady who lives on the ground floor of Miss Josie's house. She can see the whole street from her window. Does she look out the window? No, sits on the front public steps and block the way for anybody tryin to enter or leave. Name is Miss Christopher. She won't move to let you by till you ask. Sits pat and talks other folk's business. I don't know her astrology sign, might be on a cusp and so belong to two signs. Soon as you there, she be talkin.

"Heard Emmeline's boyfriend quit her."

"Who is Emmeline?" Miss Josie ask.

"That homely-lookin, skinny gal who live near the corner, in that broke-down house. You know, the one whose father is servin time for passin bad checks."

If you wait for her to move and let you get by, you be there yet. Josie try to hint. "Well, I have to get upstairs and make buttonholes for two garments." Miss Christopher shift a little but not movin.

"Apartment Seven just went up. She still workin housework and tryin to pass for a office clerk. Always carry that briefcase and dress like a secretary. God knows all about it. You can't fool God. He know what she is—with or without the briefcase."

"Miss Christopher, please let me by."

"Gladly, why didn't you say?" She not ready to move yet. "What you cookin for dinner?"

Josie tries to squeeze by. "Oh, first one thing and then another."

"Way you do . . . I bet any fool a dollar . . . you havin *lobster.*"

"Maybe I will, Miss Christopher, just so you won't lose your money."

Miss Christopher laugh kinda sick. "You too much." But she moved.

After we got away from her I whisper, "That lady needs her consciousness raise."

Josie toss her head like those under Gemini sometime do. "She needs to raise her backside off the stoop so people can pass. She also needs a lock-type zipper for her big, destructive mouth."

13. JOSEPHINE

I searched for my tape measure over an hour. It was hanging around my neck. Found it when I looked in the bedroom mirror. Father Time has done a tap dance on my face. All the moisturizer they make can't erase the wrinkle damage done by my angry mind. I pause now and then to give myself an encouraging pat on the back. "You're okay, Josephine." Many, in my fix, take their problems to the psychiatrist's couch. I can't afford it. I get through the day by planning in advance . . . put on slippers, now robe . . . say "Good morning, Rainbow." . . . Hurry to bathroom before she asks questions. Turn on shower . . . adjust water temperature . . . wait . . . take off clothing . . . get in shower, turn face up to the water. Turn off shower . . . get out . . . towel . . . dress. I follow my charted course like an old slave sailing ship, full of sadness. A bit more speed for dealing with others . . . rest . . . speed . . . more rest . . . then speed. I do very well, no one notices I'm sick. Just can't stand up to being noticed. Make way and let me ease on by. Don't look, don't question, let me ease on by. I'm no trouble, mean no harm . . . let me pass.

My appointment book helps. Everything written down for the day, the job . . . the time . . . the place. Each garment has the name pinned to it. It takes planning. A doctor might order bed-rest . . . or an ocean voyage. A prescription for heartache. I'm too poor to take advantage of either one and a bit too rich to apply for free services. This trying time would be the moment when I'm responsible for another human being. Well, maybe it's a blessing. Rainbow might be my "treatment."

"Miss Josephine, today's Monday. Tomorrow is my deadline for bringin a parent to school."

"Say bring*ing*. You write compositions in good English. Speak that way."

"I like to sound like my friends. Nobody wants me bringin them strange sounds."

"Say bring*ing*."

"Yes, mam, bring*ing*. If Kathie is not back in time . . . will you come tell Miss Paloma you're my aunt?"

"Your mother promised to be here."

"She will . . . but I mean if somethin happen."

"Nothing will happen."

"If it does, will you go say you my aunt?"

"No need to get loud about it. No, I will not. I detest a liar."

Tried to keep that snappish tone out of my voice . . . but there it is again. She puts on her persecuted look. "Didn't mean to bug you, Miss Josie. If nobody shows, it'll make me the onliest one who hasn't had a parent-teacher evaluation."

"Don't say 'onliest.' You will be the *only* one, not the 'onliest.' "

"Last night you said . . . 'I feel like the loneliest woman in town.' If you can be the loneliest, how come I can't be the onliest?"

"We'll figure that out when you're not in a hurry to be off to school. I will write a note and explain your situation."

"I'm not a situation and I don't feel like being explained."

Rainbow is becoming rude now that Kathie's whereabouts are known. When her mother called she sounded relaxed and unconcerned as usual. She knows the child is safe; she may never return. I'm ticking off clients' appointments one by one. In a few minutes, I hope, she'll go on to school. I'll read over Hal's letters again. There's one space where I can now retire . . . my bedroom. It used to be *our* bedroom. Never before have I had a room of my own. As a child, there were two brothers and a sister. For the first time, I can enter a room and close the door . . . call it mine. The sewing room off the kitchen is not that. Rainbow's room is the dining area with only a screen divider.

When Hal was here my main privacy was locked boxes and one locked drawer. "Josie, sweet," he'd say, "I can't see in the mirror for all of your music and jewelry boxes. I know you don't have this much jewelry." I have a small cedar chest which serves as a "closet" for my special mail. His old love letters, foreign cards from traveling clients. My mother's silver necklace-watch. There's a velvet-lined box, on the top is a plastic carousel of gray horses turning a circle. Mrs. Anderson gave me that. There's also a standing box which I keep on the living room cupboard . . . it's two feet tall. There are travel brochures inside . . . all the places we meant to go . . . Senegal, Egypt, India. Inside my dresser drawer is a flat box of black wood with brass decorations, a unicorn in a garden. It cost forty-three dollars in the Paris flea market. Inside are snapshots and postcards we collected during our ten-day stay. I was so proud that we went when we really couldn't afford it . . . and in April!

"Miss Josie, I have to go now."

Her sweet self again, no frowns. Such a beautiful girl. Milk-and-coffee complexion, velvety dark eyes. I wish she knew she's good-looking. Her hair is coming undone. "Rainbow, fix your hair. You're attractive, so why act as if you're not." She pins her hair with a broken barrette. Wish I had not spoken. Every time I open my mouth out comes a correction. She gazes at me with compassion . . . a motherly look. She leans over me . . . for permission.

"Can I go to Teen Canteen after school? Everybody can do the 'New York' except me. There's gonna be a dance instructor. Miss Josie, please?"

"Yes, you may. I have to pick up lace seam binding and three yards of brocade. Wouldn't you like to go with me and pick out blouse material . . ."

"You just said I could go to disco."

"Home before dark? Word of honor?"

"Okay."

No sense in shutting out every joy. Makes me such a villain. Mayola always speaks up for Rainbow. "You have to allow the child a certain freedom." Even Rachel hints. "Don't hold the girl with too short a rein." So happens they are not responsible for her. I am the guardian. People resent being cared for and guarded . . . even resent

being helped and loved. However, Harold Lamont can
go to hell on a hot day and turn on the steam heat . . .
as far as I'm concerned.

"Miss Josie, when Kathie gets home she's givin me
money to have my hair relaxed . . . that way I won't
have to comb out snarls and tangles every day. Gonna
look neat all the time. I'd rather have braids and
beads . . . but relax is neat and . . . cheaper."

"That's fine . . . Rainey. Take care, and enjoy danc-
ing."

"Sure will."

Door opens, closes, footsteps fade away . . . she's
gone. I bathe my eyes in cold water. Review the tasks in
my appointment book. Such a pretty book with a
tapestry-type cover. The museum sells lovely calendars
and desk sets. Each page has a thought for the day. Today
it is "Forgive and forget." Been hearing it all my life.
The forgive part is easy. How do I learn to forget? I never
forget anything except . . . like where I put my tape
measure. "Forgive and forget." I write it on a sheet of
paper, then tape it to the kitchen cabinet. It will be my
meditation for the day. When I shut my eyes . . . Hal's
face is before me, I hear his voice.

"It's over, Josie, not your fault . . . It's just over."

Forgetting takes practice. I forgive Hal. I write "Forgive
and *forget*" on another paper . . . for *my* room. I think
of Rainbow. "If you can be the *loneliest* . . . why can't
I be the *onliest?*" Indeed, that's exactly what we are, only
and lonely. I read and reread Hal's last letter. From room
to room, my reminders remind . . . FORGIVE AND FOR-
GET.

Pick up clothes and hang in the closet . . . FORGIVE

AND FORGET . . . Wash dishes and dry . . . FORGIVE AND
FORGET . . . Open the cabinet, put away cups . . . FOR-
GIVE AND FORGET

Forgive and forget. Something is missing. Where is
Rainbow's key? There's an empty space—she has taken
the key to her mother's apartment. It was there last night.
Why take a key to go to the disco? Maybe I moved it and
forgot. No, I didn't. She has taken the key. Forgive and
forget—she has definitely taken the key.

14. RAINBOW

Eljay stayed on my case. One day he wouldn't sit with me in cafeteria. Actin friendly but hangin out with a girl name Janine. Tryin to make me jealous so I'll see things his way. Talkin with her but kept lookin at me to see how I take it. After school he waited on the corner till I walk by.

"Hey, Rainey!"

"What?"

"You tryin to igg me?"

"Me? Look like you the one found new company."

"Let's talk."

"If you wanta."

We sit on the park bench and he's singin the same song. "Girl, you got hang-ups bout sex. Nothin wrong with sex. It's a natural thing. If a guy don't get off, once in a while, like his health'll be broke. You can injure yourself from holdin back feelins. Can get a hernia."

I don't like bein asked to make love to save his health. Make me feel like I'm the Red Cross or Cancer Aid. No matter how "natural" he say sex is . . . I'm thinkin Kathie would kill me to death if she find out I'm into that.

Told me many times . . . "You ever be in trouble, I'll skin you alive!" I told Eljay, "If I get pregnant nothin for me to do but leave town!" He was lookin so fine in his tan check Sherlock Holmes hat and the burnt orange T-shirt with brown corduroy slacks. His parents both got city jobs and he's wearin the latest at all times. I sometime wonder what he want with me a-tall cause my wardrobe is like nowhere. Miss Josie made me a plaid skirt and vest. Fit nice. I appreciate it but what I really want is a African print top to go over "Honey Buns" . . . that's what'll go good when I someday get my beaded braids with seashells.

"Rainey, somethin sick bout pettin and kissin right up to ready, then turn it off. Buster told me to forget you cause you never gonna come through."

"How Buster know what we do or don't do?"

"He ask and I level with him, that's how."

"Should tell him nothin!"

"What's the secret? We into Sex Ed., right? What's the use knowin how everything happens if you not ever suppose to do it?"

"Eljay, some people mature sooner than others."

"You look more mature than lotta girls, Rainey. I get wet dreams."

"Nightly emissions will not do any harm. Like Miss Townes say, it's nature's way of relievin our tensions."

"Emissions? Say wet dreams. Sex Ed. use lotta dumb words and names for things. Foolin around is 'foreplay,' comin is 'ejaculation.' Talk that way outside-a class and everybody be laughin at your ignorance. Townes call screwin . . . 'coitus.' Nother thing, nobody in history ever had to hold sex classes for giraffes or lions. No discussion needed. They don't have-ta name parts-a they genitals."

"You not a giraffe or a lion."

"I'm wise. They can get some satisfaction while I can't."

I'm still holdin out. Kissin and just feelin good goes a long way with me. I wouldn't mind makin him happy and savin his health if it was somethin I could tell people . . . like "we went to the show" or "out to lunch." I'd like to feel free enough to tell anybody . . . Kathie, Miss Josie . . . even Miss Rachel. Maybe I'm not as hot-natured as some people. I try to explain to him but he's stubborn.

"Rainey, you might be a dyke-lesbian who don't yet know it. Girl, you could be ruinin your true nature."

Eljay talks too much bout bodily function and not enough bout *love*. I'm wonderin if he really loves me. Always gotta ask to get him to say it. "Eljay, do you truly love me?"

"Why you keep askin? I *told* you but you make me repeat. Do you love *me*? That's the real question. I'm the one willin to give myself to you but you the one who don't feel the same."

"I do want to but . . . I love you, I need you— but—"

"What's the 'but'?"

"Everybody say Beryl is pregnant and Buster not gonna marry her. She's the one left with the trouble."

He gets up and hikes his belt like he's uncomfortable. Walkin up and down to one side like plannin to go off and leave me there. He say, "One thing, Beryl's regular enough to go on and have a baby without complainin.

She facin the music like a stone woman."

"Maybe she's too young to be havin a baby."

"If that was so . . . she wouldn't be pregnant. But she facin the music like a stone woman."

"What is Buster facin?"

"Beryl's parents gonna keep the baby and she goin back to finish school, no sweat."

I didn't want Eljay to walk away. Suppose *nobody* ever loves me? Worse yet . . . when the rest be paired off in couples .. . . I'll be alone, the left-out one.

Seems like my mouth won't stop. "I'd like to finish school first."

He smile a little kinder. "Why not?" he say. "Beryl had a accident, okay? A slip-up. There's things to do to keep from havin a baby. I know a few myself. You can go to a control clinic and get pills. Doctors also give out something you can wear. Sex education teacher might even tell you."

"I'm not gonna ask her, Eljay. She might tell my mother."

"No, they suppose to be confidential like how when somebody goes to the votin booth and cast a vote."

"Would you go with me to a doctor? I'd spend my hair-braid money."

"I wouldn't mind . . . but what for? You the one gonna wear whatever it is."

"Eljay, what about . . . er . . . condoms?"

"Rubbers old-timey. That's to prevent disease. We not diseased. If I must . . . I must . . . but it's square. What's wrong with withdrawal?"

"That's call interrupted coitus. Might not be dependable."

"Coitus . . . square talk."

"I read where a man had a *vasectomy* . . . right in the doctor's office . . . just like how people go to the dentist."

"Girl, you crazy? That's a operation!"

Look like his eyes fillin with tears. I didn't really mean for him to go have a operation, was just talkin bout what I heard. "Gee, Eljay . . . there's always like . . . you know . . . what's call abstinence." I tried to kiss him and he turn away.

"Stop kiddin around. Buster is right. Must be that I just don't turn you on."

"You do, you do . . . but . . ."

"But, but, it's but with you all the way. I don't wanta push you inta anything if you too chicken to make a womanly move."

He wave "so long," straighten his Sherlock Holmes and walk off. He got the most stylish walk of any boy I know.

It was not easy to watch him hangin round with Janine. Not many girls can be prettier. She got long curly hair. Girl name Veronica told me how Janine's hair is not natural but that she use relaxer to straighten it. What's the difference? Hair bounces round like a shampoo commercial. Janine wear high-high heels on ankle-strap shoes, got a see-through blouse . . . with no bra to cut the view. The blouse is pinky-brown and so are her tits. You gotta look real hard to know what she's showin . . . but she got everybody lookin. She's stark-buck naked underneath that blouse. Her jeans so tight she gotta lie down to zip em up. Came in the school bathroom while I was in there. No doors on the toilets. Had to pull the jeans down below her knees so she could squat. Doesn't wear panties underneath the jeans. She act like she's thirty and I'm pre-school kindergarten. We both the same, fourteen.

"Goin to canteen, little sugar?"

I don't answer. She flash all thirty-two of her big teeth in a Gleem smile and ask, "Mind if I go dancin with Eljay?"

"What's it to me?"

"Good girl," she say. "We not to let these men drive us up the wall or go to hair-pullin. I don't like to move into another chick's territory so I check it out up front. If you got your name on him just holler and I won't latch on."

"Make me no difference."

"Good girl. You the one drew that vagina in sex class, right?"

"I'm the one."

"That was cute. You draw nice."

She dipped her comb under the cold water faucet, combin water through her hair and shakin it back like a rodeo horse tryin to throw his rider. "See you later, doll."

Janine walked out, makin noise with the high heels. Left me standin, feelin simple.

Janine kept it up all week. I went to canteen off and on. Stayin away would make me look bad. Goin was worse. She and Eljay danced. He lift her up and then threw her under his legs. Janine kick so high till everybody had to applaud. She can make people cheer whenever she want them to. Me, I smiled like bein a good sport. Fact is, I started the applause. She brought Eljay over and say . . . "Dance with Rainey so I can cool off and catch my breath. Give them a hand!" Janine hollered, as he led me out on the floor. Nobody bothered.

I went in the powder room to duck the ones who were

glad to see me sad. A girl name Veronica followed me . . . "Rainey, don't let that tramp take your guy. That's all I say. Everybody gonna laugh you outta town if you take this."

I wrote a note and sneaked it in his hand. "Eljay, come have lunch with me at my mother's house on Monday. I will be *alone* . . . Rainey." He read it and gave a smile and a wink. She watched us, also smilin. But I didn't care.

15. RAINBOW

No turnin back now. I won't change my mind. I'm walkin away from my old self, becomin a new person. People all say how sex is nothin but a natural function. To me it was seemin too important. A shy person is just shy . . . but I shouldn't be. Today, for the first time, I cut school. Walked around for an hour fore I came home and put the key in my mother's lock. Walked along the outside-a the park. Would have liked to go inside but a girl was raped in there . . . and killed. Rape is a terrible form of sex. In school, Miss Townes say that the wrong kinda sex and all kindsa violence is because of bad movies. The R movies showin almost much as Beryl's book on "Ninety Sex Positions." There's R, X, PG and G movies. "PG" stand for "parental guidance." You can go in to see those without any question. They figure how if you showed up it must be okay with your parent. To truly "guide," the parent would have to go see the picture first. Adults don't too much go for PG pictures . . . they rather see R. I've never seen a X. But me and Eljay have bought tickets and just walk on into the R ones. Nobody ask nothin but to take our money. R is suppose to be for seventeen and over. Sex must suddenly seem different when you turn seventeen.

If it's such a natural thing, how come everybody actin weird about it? I saw a R picture where this girl, not lookin no older than me, turned her naked behind right up to the camera. Man sittin next to me was suckin in his breath, moanin and gaspin in a disgustin way. Beryl and I had to get up and move to another seat. He reminded me of a repairman who tried to take advantage and feel my bosom. I had asked him to please close a window in the school hall. If he had made a pass or *ask* me somethin . . . I coulda dealt with that and turn him off. He was sneaky, act like doin some awful thing. Sure wasn't thinkin nothin beautiful bout sex. He was ready to brute-out!

True love is mostly featured in fairy tales. Sleepin Beauty put off sex for a hundred years. When a prince finally did find her . . . he kiss her *gently*, then they gallop off on a pretty horse so they could enjoy the happy-ever-after. They never mentioned sex. Neither one studied the structure of the penis. Miss Townes showed us plaster forms of a baby in the womb. In each form the baby is a bit larger until it's big enough to labor out and be born. Poor thing must feel like gettin an eviction. Bet that's why a baby cries first thing. Cinderella never had to deal with sex, it was nowhere in the story. People long ago used to fall in love without havin to make sex decisions.

Well, time for me to live in the real world like everybody else. Kathie wasn't but fifteen when I was born. I try not to think of that during Sex Ed. class. Girls were talkin bout how old their mothers were when they were

born . . . nineteen was the youngest age I heard. I put
Kathie's age up to twenty. Sex and the society turns me
stone chicken.

I do not wanta undo my jeans in front of Eljay. I wear
a almost naked bikini to swim pool, but that's different.
Natives in a tropical country wouldn't have much to take
off for sex; maybe just lift some beads or leaves to one
side. Kathie's robe is still on her chair. I could strip and
wear that . . . so I'd be ready. I can't put on her robe
. . . be like takin unfair advantage while she's away. She
has a caftan in the closet. That's different . . . not as
bed-timey as a robe.

Shower felt fine. Five-day underarm deodorant. No
sweat. Hair combed out looks better than braids . . .
fluffy. House slippers look too beat. So what's wrong with
bare feet? Kathie's Shalimar smells good. In Social Studies there's this place they say Margaret Mead lived with
natives. The single girls wore a flower over one ear,
moved it to the other when they got engaged. Was it the
left or right ear? A paper rose seems kinda tacky. I'll die
if Eljay laughs. This is sure serious . . . like my favorite
commercial song . . . "Peak Freans are a very serious cookie . . . If you're a grown-up or plan to be
one . . ."

In the bottom dresser drawer are the good sheets . . .
for sickness. My mother is prepared for sickness, if we
not sick too long. Two sets with white embroidery and
initial J. Maybe there's somethin I can teach Eljay bout
sex . . . the beauty. My body is okay . . . little too round
but not bad. Janine is so long-legged, yet with broad
shoulders and good breasts. But Cinderella and Sleepin
Beauty were not drawn that way by the artists who drew

them for books. They were rounder, like me. Enough
of childhood thinkin . . . this is now, and as Miss Paloma say, "Every age has its beauty."

Lunch . . . tuna sandwiches and R.C. Cola . . . also
one pretty red apple. He can have it. Wonder if lunch
should be first or after? Better *after*. Lunch might make
me belch . . . or somethin. Guess that's why the prince
always snatched up the princess and ran away at the end
of the story . . . so the storyteller would not have to deal
with details. It is possible to plan too much and get stuff
wrong. There are also some "what ifs." What if my
mother walks in and catches us? If she doesn't kill me
I'll say . . . "Kathie, this is my fault, not Eljay's. I'm a
woman and not anymore a girl. I'm sorry to make you
lose faith in me." If she goes violent I'll run down the
fire-escape exit and give Eljay the chance to escape
through the front. What a dumb-lookin end to a heavy
love scene. And what if Eljay happens not to be turned
on? Suppose he's cooled off? Well, he'd better not plan
a return engagement. I couldn't go through this another
time. I look nice . . . much as I can. Got a disc ready
to play . . . "Do It for Me Now" . . . that's his song
. . . got fine back-up singers too.

Time is now quarter to one. That's another "what if."
What if he doesn't show? In that case I'd pretend I hadn't
been here either. Eljay, Eljay, Eljay, don't let me down.
Down? I "center down." Don't know if God belongs in
this . . . but I'm prayin for a good "first time." God,
please let it be okay. Feel ashamed askin God to supervise
sex . . . but I see prizefighters prayin God to help them
beat up somebody in the ring. Doesn't let me off the
hook. How can a person cut school to sneak sex, then

pray for it to go good? Mainly prayin not to get pregnant. Poor little Jesus' mother must have gone through some bad days. She gave birth without sex . . . called immaculate. Some people maybe didn't believe her and say, "That child look like a ordinary sex-baby to me even if he is name Jesus." People can be mean. They gossip about my mother. They always like somebody to chew on . . . long as it's not themselves. Still centerin down . . . God, help me not to feel like dyin if he doesn't show . . . or if he does. There's our bell that Kathie bought last Christmas . . . sweet-soundin two-chime . . . sound like sayin "Hel-lo." Kathie like nice sounds.

I turn on the music . . . "Do It for Me Now" . . . soft and easy. I hold the paper rose since I'm not sure over what ear to put it. I open the door and throw open my arms the way Miss Josephine do. Eljay is standin there . . . and JANINE with him. My arms up and out for welcome . . . she's standin with a funny grin on her face . . . speakin even before he does. "Look like you just got up, honey!"

He's actin stupid. "Say, Rainey, er . . . maybe how bout another time?"

But Janine dances on in, doin shake-butt steps to my music. "Come on, Eljay-baby, do it!"

He sound sick while explainin, "Janine ask me go help her pick out new shoes. Took more time than we plan. Had to make out papers to put em on layaway . . . they snakeskin. We had some lunch." I'm thinkin she's snake enough to make shoes outta her own skin. Some other fool is now talkin . . . must be me.

"Don't run. There's sandwiches and soda . . . I . . . I ate. Why don't you and Janine sit down . . ."

I'm actin like Miss Josephine, or is it Mrs. Anderson? I know I'm not me.

He says, "No jive, Rainey, we don't want anything."

She can't stop shakin and goin back and forth all around him. "Eljay-baby, Rainey'll be mad if we let her goodies go to waste. Let's cut the rest-a the afternoon and celebrate my birthday!"

Janine takes the rose outta my hand and slips it in her hair. He looks surprised. "Neeney, I didn't know this was your birthday."

"It's not, lover, I just wanta celebrate it . . . that way it won't be takin up extra time when it get here. That's how I party . . . in advance."

He's lookin at her like she's Diana Ross. I'm waitin on them, glad not to sit down. He eats both sandwiches; she bites the apple. "Sister, you smell so good. What's your perfume?"

"Shalimar."

"Get it. Lemmie try some on."

He tryin to make a compliment. "Rainey, you er . . . you sure turn out boss sandwiches. Bet you know how to fry chicken and make potato salad."

Janine is spittin apple skins into the napkin. "Eljay-baby, bet she knows what to do with anything that goes in a pot. Rainbow is a natural *sister*!"

He plays "Do It for Me Now" three times. They dancin the "bump," hip to hip, finger poppin, smilin at each other. I exuse myself to go to the bathroom and splash water on my face. I'm holdin on to the water faucet, tryin not to cry. Janine pushes the door open . . . pulls down her jeans below the knee, squats over the toilet and splashes the seat. Now takin over the basin to wash her hands with my brand-new bar-a gardenia soap. Now dryin on the prettiest guest towel . . . embroidery like a bouquet of blue flowers. I'm wishin they will leave while I still got some cool.

"Rainey, you a real down sister. You what I call a good sport. You know how to turn a stud loose. That's classy, cold cool you got. When things be over they over, right?"

"That's right."

"Gotta come by my house sometime. No need in lettin a nigga break up two sisters. He cute though . . . smooth. But I don't have-ta tell you."

I'm wonderin if they'll *ever* go. The back-up singers goin "do it . . . do it . . . do it." Janine, hands on hips, seem ready to snatch Eljay and make love in front-a me.

Now I turn into Kathie . . . can't handle this and be Josie or Barbara Anderson. "Move on. Get out. I had enough of it and I'm tired-a hearin the same record over and over."

"You want us to play another one?"

"No, Janine. How does the sayin go? Exit, let the doorknob hitcha where the good Lord splitcha!"

Eljay pullin her to go. "Neeney, let's make it on out."

She goin for power. "Baby, maybe I oughta go and leave you two alone to settle whatever's wrong."

He's pickin up his Sherlock Holmes and movin on with her. "Neeney, ain't nothin wrong. I'm with you."

"Seem like Miss Rainbow wanta act like she's better than us. We nothin and she's all."

"That's right. I am better. Far as I'm concern . . . yall just two shits lookin at a rose."

"Sister Jordan, if you hard-up for a man, be my guest. You can have him if he wanta stay!"

Got her hands on her hips and pattin one foot like
she's ready to give me a beatin. I just raise my head like
Miss Josephine. "I'm careful who I sleep behind; that's
how people catch disease. You two deserve nothin better
than each other." I fluff my hair with my hands, lettin
them both know that if there's a Diana Ross in the room
. . . it's me. Her face turn dark red . . . while he pull
her through the door. I slam the lock shut . . . and it's
over.

I been sittin here on the floor for a long time. So mad
and ashamed . . . couldn't keep my cool. Didn't stay
centered down. I had made up my mind to see it
through, then shake hands and say so long till another
time. Why couldn't I be Mrs. Anderson? Now they both
know I was jealous. It's all worse than it was before.
They'll be tellin everybody. Be awful to walk back in
class with people knowin . . . "Eljay broke her heart and
left her for Janine."

One set-a footsteps walk up to the door. There's the
bell . . . "Hel-lo" . . . Would either of em have the
nerve to come back? Maybe one is hidin while the other
ring. If they tell me off I'll have to take it. Got no more
fight left. Not gonna answer.

"Rainbow . . . answer the door. I know you're in
there. You took the key and I know it. Answer the door.
If you don't answer I'll call the agency. Why make trouble? You want Mayola to call your mother? Child, please
open the door. You are worrying me to death."

I let Miss Josie in. First thing, she goes through the
rooms lookin. After she sees there's no one else, she
. . . lingers in front of the bed made up with new, pretty
sheets.

"Girl, what have you been up to? I hope you haven't

been doing anything your mother would not approve. . ."

Hard to answer. I don't wanta be Kathie or Barbara Anderson or Miss Josie or Miss Rachel. I don't even wanta be Diana Ross. I wanta be myself . . . but I don't know how. All I know is bout other people . . . there's nothin to know bout me; if there is . . . I just don't know it.

Miss Josie has looked at the table with the plates on it bout five times. She takes my hand and leads me back to the bedroom . . . lookin at the new sheets all pretty.

"I'm glad the bed has not been slept in."

"Are you?"

Miss Josie look old and sick. She forgot to fix her face with makeup. She hold my shoulders so hard till seem like her fingers gonna reach down to the bone.

"Don't lie to me, Rainbow. I want the truth. I deserve the truth."

I tell the truth. "Those the prettiest sheets we own. Kathie keep them for sickness . . . so if a doctor have-ta come or a ambulance or like that . . . we be lookin presentable. Eljay has been wantin to make love to me . . . I could wait but he could not. But I wanted him too."

"He tried to take advantage. Did he?"

"No, mam. I asked him here. He brought his new girlfriend with him. I put on my mother's caftan . . . I waited for him to come and go to bed with me. He brought his new girlfriend."

"I'm glad."

"Sorry you glad. It broke my heart."

"Child, you're better off than you know."

"You know that, I don't."

"Lovely sheets . . . you should be able to use them
without sickness or . . . lovemaking . . ."

"Miss Josie, please don't explain me no more about
life . . . Please stop. All I want is nothin, like nothin."

She doesn't know what "stop" is about. All the way
home she's after makin me admit things. "Rainbow, I
truly hope there's been no intimacy with that boy. I hope
you've been truthful because I'll be held accountable to
your mother, the agency, to Mayola."

"Tell em whatever you want. I told you the truth. I
asked him to be intimate . . . but he was not interested.
You make me say it over and over . . . He did not want
me, okay?"

"Only reason I keep asking is because you lied to me
about the key. You promised not to touch the key."

"I lied to you. I took the key. I was wrong."

"Over and over I've placed my trust in you."

"Yes, mam, you placed your trust."

"Why did you lie?"

"I don't know."

"Promise this will not happen again . . . and I won't
report to Mayola or your mother."

"I'm not promisin you or anybody anything. Report
what you want. I'm a bad person, okay?"

"Well, this time the key will be *locked* away. The
honor system does not work."

"Right, forget honor."

They all know how to draw blood just like ten machine
guns bein fired at me all at once. I got news for Miss
Townes, who so busy teachin death and sex studies. She
don't know what death and sex is all about. Ask me.

Josephine Lamont can't stop runnin her mouth. She's

on me all the way home. Sometime I'm in front, other times she is. I drop back or move forward, anything but walkin side by side. My one ambition is to have nobody talkin bout how I oughta be.

"Rainbow, I'm only trying to protect you."

She knows a thousand ways to say the same thing. "You have made me lose trust . . ."

I'm not gonna repeat myself anymore. Silence is a mean-ass weapon that some people deserve to have used on them. She's not the one who has to hit school and get the bad-mouthin that's waitin for me. When Eljay and Janine get through with my name I may's well move to Alaska. They probably know folks there too. One thing, I'll never get to be runner-up in the Miss America. You might twirl the hell outta that baton or sing from a opera . . . but a bad-mouthin will keep you outta everything. How can I walk in class tomorrow and keep my cool? How I'm gonna sit in on Sex Education? People gonna ride me like a roller coaster. How I'm gonna face parent-teacher evaluation and Kathie not there?

Josephine Lamont jawin right up to the house, then . . . "I forgot to buy seam binding. Care to come along to the variety store?" Me, I don't wanta go noplace.

"I'll wait out here on the steps till you get back."

"Here, you can use my key." She drops it in my lap.

"No, thank you, I will wait."

"Would you like to visit Rachel?"

"No, I say I'll wait."

"Go upstairs. I didn't mean what I said about losing trust."

"I will wait right here, okay?"

She had to go on and quit buggin me.

I'm sittin mindin my business. Here come Miss Christopher to take her usual place in front-a the entrance.

"How you doin, baby doll?"

"Fine, how you doin?"

"As well as the Lord allows. Poor Josephine. She's walkin slower nowdays. Don't let her down . . . Stick with her. She thinks more of you than some the others she took in. Don't leave her."

"She just miss Mr. Hal. He'll soon come back from visitin his relatives."

"Visitin relatives? That man *left* her. Everybody round here know he ran off with the woman who run the beauty parlor . . . 'The Gilded Hand.' Harold Lamont is a *womanizer*. Can't too much blame him in a way-a speakin. Josephine is at least five years older than he is. He mighta *had* to fool with that beautician. Course, if a man leave me, I'd just forget him. She worryin herself into a decline. This new one he got, Cordelia, only bout half his age. He use to keep books and do accountin for her. She close down shop and they done run off. When a woman gettin old she can't hold up like she use-ta. Josephine won't face facts. She refuse to go on over the hill and give up. Josephine is too vain. Vanity will kill you. A man, at any age, got it made. A woman is different. You take for a instance my cousin . . ."

I step over her, without lookin back.

She grab me by the jeans. "Hold on, sugar lump. I got a letter from him to her. It's postmark West Palm Beach, Florida . . . but got no return address. How bout that? The postman drop it in my box by mistake. You give her this letter and don't repeat what I said. No use to hurt her little feelins. She been givin me the cold shoulder of late. I never done her nothin but kindness, God is my judge. But Harold Lamont is a womanizer and bein rude to me won't make him a bit better."

I open the door . . . the place look like robbers tore it up. Boxes and brown envelopes open on the dining room table . . . all that boxed stuff she's forever lockin in drawers. Sign on the fridge door . . . "Forgive and forget". . . A trail-a letters, pictures and postcards every-where. Her passport on the coffee table. I pick up that passport and look the hell right in it . . . I don't have any privacy either. Talk bout lyin. How could she make out like he's doin real estate for some sick cousin? Pass-port is blue with gold print. Her picture inside look like a criminal photo hangin in the post office. Hello, again . . . my math is good enough to see she is *fifty-seven* . . . seven years past the half century she boast about. Lies on top-a lies, but want truth outta me. I'm pickin up travel brochures and takin in her bedroom to respect-fully place on her bedspread . . . along with letters. Not readin through like how she went in my suitcase and remove "Ninety Sex Positions." Her dresser drawer . . . her *secret* drawer . . . is unlock. Lotta crap . . . moisture cream, false eyelashes, and two bottles-a hair dye . . . Brown/Charcoal Special. She got a little music box. I wind it up . . . it play "Love Story." This woman worse than the Frankenstein monster.

I pull out the big dresser drawer all the way. Didn't she go in my suitcase. She got a lace see-thru nightie that make Janine's blouse look like a nun's outfit. Even own *bleach* cream. How bout somebody who read BLACK poetry and also use bleach cream? Oh, I'm seein her. This the lady Mayola say would make a good "role

model." Uh-huh, also got a brand-new frosted lipstick
and a eyeliner.

Josephine Lamont come walkin into the room . . .
look like she don't know whether to shit or shout. Don't
need bleach now. She already turn one shade lighter. I
hand over his letter.

"Miss Christopher give me this to give you from Mr.
Lamont. She say the postman drop it in her box."

She take the letter and sit down on the bed . . . holdin
it . . . lookin at me with tears rollin down, like I'm the
one doin her wrong . . . not the "womanizer."

"No, oh, no, Rainbow, no, no . . ."

I ain't sad or sorry. The true me is comin out at last.
I'm glad, happy like it's Christmas Eve. Whose life is a
lie now? She's grabbin up all the letters and travel folders
scatter over her satin quilt. Rockin back and forth, cryin
and holdin the stuff.

"I didn't read any letters, Mrs. Lamont. All I looked
at was your passport . . . and it was open."

While she rockin and cryin . . . I'm rememberin Miss
Paloma once sayin . . . "The wheels of God grind
slowly, yet they grind exceeding small." Which is another way of sayin . . . "What goes around comes
around." You judge somebody else and your own judg-
ment will come home to roost. People in glass houses
are the ones who throw stones. I gotta say it. "Answer
me this, Miss Josephine, how come respect must all go
one way and not the other?"

She still starin and rollin down tears. Tryin to make
somebody sorry for her by actin pitiful. Gatherin her silly
stuff and stashin it back in boxes . . . puttin away the
passport. One thing for sure, my mother never lie about

age. Kathie Jordan know how to talk straight truth to a
judge in a courtroom. This woman lyin when nobody
forcin her to do it. I never *ask* her age! Dyes her hair,
that's another lie when you look at it a certain way.

I got a question. "Miss Josie, why you say your age is
fifty when it is fifty-*seven*?"

"I guess cause there's not much in my bankbook
. . . maybe I knew I'd be alone, like now . . . with very
short funds."

"But you *got* a bankbook. We *never* had any except
for Christmas Club . . . Kathie let that run out. We only
collected twenty dollars stead-a the fifty. It would-a paid
full if she had deposit every week. Why boo-hoo bout
bankbooks?"

"Rainbow, I'm self-employed, not old enough for any
kind of pension, not young enough to retire . . . or to
find somebody who will spend the rest of the time with
me. You're a child. You don't know."

This is goin down too rough on her . . . but it is phony
not to face up. After all, if somebody wants out . . . let
them go. Didn't I let Eljay go to Janine? Bad as I went
on . . . I never ask him not to leave. And he better not
ever ask to come back. I can take bein left and Miss Josie
can't. What's the way to bow out? Like a fallin star in
the midnight blue. Fade away leavin a bright glow. Just
don't try to fool yourself. Put-downs will hurt anybody's
feelins but I wait till night comes, when I can tuck my
head under the bed cover . . . so I can cry one to one,
me to myself. A bankbook is no answer to lyin bout age.

"Miss Josie, what good is it to take off seven years?"

"I gain a little more time to enjoy life . . . and love
a little longer."

"But you don't have the seven. You not really foolin anybody."

"Fooled you, didn't I?"

"Yeah, but I'm only fourteen . . . not wise to the ways."

"You'll learn as time goes by. You're hammering a nail through my heart. Let's stop."

There's lots for her to learn right now. "Miss Josie, plenty old people findin happiness. They content to be makin pies and visitin the sick. They not thinkin bout makin love and like that. They sit in the best part-a the bus . . . like it say 'save this seat for the elderly and the handicapped.' "

She lookin at me like I'm three. Wipe her eyes and seemin amuse. "Some old folks pretending bout pies and good deeds being enough. Wanting to love and be loved . . . never stops. They *pretend* it does to win approval from those who are younger. It's a sad joke. Our faces and bodies no longer match our thoughts and desires."

Now she's studyin the false eyelashes, bleach and hair dye. I'm hopin she'll throw the stuff in the wastebasket . . . show some style. She's puttin it all back in the drawer. Bleach cream is still out. She opens the jar, takes a dab, then massagin her hands. She say . . . "Unfortunately how we look has a lot to do with drawing lovers and friends. As we fade, people grow rude . . . and we become meek and foolish."

"Not everybody, Miss Josie. Lotta elderly have dignity. Miss Townes say people should grow old gracefully."

She's feelin her letter from Hal . . . not openin it, just feelin and turnin with her bleach-cream hands. "Rainbow, no one is expected to grow older *gracefully* before middle age. Grace is suddenly demanded when we are old, when we are weakest, when we have the least money . . . and face death. That's the time when we are told to live gracefully. My dear, maybe 'grace' should be practiced all along the way. Why wait until youth is gone? Rainbow, you could try a little grace now and then."

"Miss Josie, I know bout age. When I was little, folks would rave bout how 'cute' I was. Now, at fourteen, I get on they nerves. Except for men. They begin to look at my legs . . ."

"Like how Harold used to.look at them?"

"I didn't say that. He never got outta line or nothin."

"I know, he just looked and thought."

"Miss Josie, every age gotta be some kinda new setup. Like I'm fourteen only this one time. Soon's I get used to it . . . time to move on to fifteen . . . and like that."

I'm sorry I made her cry . . . but can't tell her straight out. She opens Mr. Hal's letter. I'm hopin he's sayin how he's sorry and wants to come back home to be with her forever.

She tosses it right over in my lap, without takin one look. "Rainbow, you're very mature today. Read it out loud . . . let me know what he's saying. Won't hurt you to hear it."

"Might be best for you to read your own mail."

"I don't have the courage. Let me hear the words . . . if you don't mind."

"Yes, mam."

First thing a check falls out. Check is for one hundred dollars. That's good for openers. Some the best days-a my life been connected with checks in the mail. I hand it over and get down to business. "Dear Josie . . . Everything remains the same. I hope you will accept our separation. Twenty years is a long time. Surely you can take most of the credit for having made them good ones. If there was anything wrong on your part, it would have made leaving easier . . ." She laugh a mean laugh and say, "Now he wants it to be *easy*. Read on."

I do. ". . . you have always been a wonderful person in every way, so good to me while I was ill and always a help to my sister and brother-in-law. They are both sorry about our break. I am too cowardly to send you my change of address. It would only make more unhappiness for both of us. The divorce, if you agree it will make it simpler. It would be well for all concerned if we arrange things as soon as possible. I'll call in a couple of weeks, after you've had time to think. Thanks for the good days. I'm willing to help you in any way, if ever I can. Write my sister. I take the liberty of signing . . . Love, Harold."

Now is really the time for her to boo-hoo, but, bein a Gemini, she smile at me like I just open a door for her. "Thank you, hearing it read makes me know it is over."

"I know how you feel. Didn't I lose Eljay?"

"You're very young. It's not the same."

"Miss Josie, hurt is hurt and losin is losin."

"You are right and . . . life goes on. What shall we attend to next?"

"Tomorrow is deadline for me to bring Kathie to school."

"She said she'd be here but maybe you shouldn't count on it."

"Whatever, don't bother Mayola."

"Mayola might have her number . . . you could call."

"I'm not gonna ask her to threaten her career . . . just to come to town and look at Miss Paloma."

"I'll call."

"No, if you call she would drop everything and be here. My father would do the same thing . . . but Leroy can't walk off his job. If they can't be here . . . they can't."

"I guess not, Rainbow."

"I know it. Kathie doesn't feel bout Burke the way you feel bout Mr. Hal. She can let any man go without crackin up."

If Josie's feelins bein hurt, that's tough. Why she start signifyin bout not to count on my mother? Now she look cool and say, "Child, you don't have to hate me in order to love your mother. Behave yourself. Don't keep putting me down to lift her up." The other side-a Gemini.

She's fast tidyin the place. All subjects closed. She serve yesterday warm-ups for supper. For the first time in ages . . . no candles on the table, not even the short stubs she burn in a saucer when there's no more long ones on hand.

I try to "pleasant" the conversation. Miss Josie always say . . . "Dinner is a time for pleasant conversation and soft lights." I don't dislike her, but somethin holds us apart. Miss Townes got a name for it . . . "generation gap." Only a small gap separates me from my mother, a bigger one from Miss Rachel; but "generation gap" kinda wide-set between me and Miss Josephine. The "gap" is in no way hate. You can love people and the gap be gettin on your nerves. Kathie's gap is weird. Like,

I know where she's comin from but I'm sort of a stranger to her. When I was nine she told a fella-friend . . . "My daughter seem like a playmate who came to visit but won't go home." He laugh and she did too. I was wonderin if she wanted me to leave.

Josie is now tryin to "pleasant" the conversation. "I will go to school with you."

"She'll show up."

"I mean if she doesn't get here."

That's the way "generation gap" like to do. They keep at a thing till it turn sickenin. People oughta know when to leave a thought alone.

Me, I change the subject. "This the first time you been without candles to burn."

"Tomorrow, when I cash the check, there'll be candles."

"I know a check-cashin place."

"I cash at the bank."

"Right. I forgot you got a bankbook."

Glad when "pleasant conversation" is over. I lay my clothes out the way she makes me. I bathe, do teeth, put up hair and make ready to face the music tomorrow. Janine and Eljay probably bad-mouthin me to the world . . . by phone. They can't kill me but they sure can make you wish you was dead. In bed I see mind pictures of me bein in South America, with foreign new people who love me and know how fine I am, people with good taste. Covers over my head and I'm not cryin . . . I'm sad mainly cause I feel sorry for Josephine. She's pitiful.

16. JOSEPHINE

Thought she would never go to bed. Lingered over every task. It's been a long day . . . sharing the break-up of my marriage with a child. It hurt, but it helped. Double failure is hard to face. Out of all the children I've taken . . . she is my greatest promise. I've eased her defiant attitude, tried to ease her hurt. I only wish she knew how smart she is. Mayola has called her mother several times to remind her about the tomorrow school meeting. True, she promised to do it, but Kathie is a "day after tomorrow" person.

I look in on Rainbow, she's asleep. The room is almost neat, clothing out for the morning. Hair braided. I've heard that it costs about seventy dollars to have hair dressed with those beads and shells. Nosy Miss Christopher knows a girl who will do it at home for thirty-five. I'm tempted to give Rainbow the money she needs to have hers done. It's all she talks about. She might resent the gift. Some "charges" absolutely refuse kindness. This child-woman keeps the little wall between us. Maybe I'm not smart enough. I've lost the man and the girl. Maybe I expect too much. I now pledge to give up correcting, reminding and pushing.

The phone rings. It's Kathie. Why would she wait until midnight? She rattles on about not being able to leave her "gig."

"Explain it for me, Josie. I can't talk to her now. You tell her how it is."

"Please come home. Rainbow needs you, Mrs. Jordan."

"I know, honey, and it's tearin me up."

"Come in for half day. Talk to the teacher. You can go back. At least talk to Rainey. I'll wake her up."

"No! Don't disturb her. My bread is runnin short . . . I paid down on a navy-blue pea-jacket for her. Tell her bout the jacket and . . . you tell that teacher to cool it. After all, she got herself a job and so have you. I'll call tomorrow . . . if I can . . ."

A click. Mrs. Katherine Jordan has hung up.

Rainbow took extra time with her morning appearance. Hope she had a good night's sleep. She doesn't stir and mash food as much as she used to . . . except when upset . . . that's often enough. She's stirring at the moment, mashing poached egg, crumbling bacon, mashing . . .

Well, since she's upset anyway. "Your mother phoned last night, after midnight."

"You didn't call me?"

"She asked me not to disturb you."

"But you know I want to be disturb."

"I asked her to come home. She hung up while I was speaking."

"She must-a been too busy like . . ."

"That's what she said. She's paid down on a navy-blue pea-jacket."

"She look nice in navy blue."

"It's for you . . . a present."

The food is now mush but she stirs on. I'm ready to go with her . . . but also tired of offering myself to others, even a child. Too long a silence. There's a bit of candle on the pantry ledge. I light it, drip wax on a saucer and stand it steady . . . almost burn my finger. She smiles. "Miss Josie, a candle for breakfast? A lit candle in the daytime when the sun is shinin?"

I sing:

> *This little light of mine*
> *I'm gonna let it shine. . . .*

She stops stirring. "Miss Josie, my mother doesn't love me as much as I love her. She never did and never will. Kathie Jordan is worse than Eljay or Mr. Hal." Floods of tears without anger . . . honest crying. "Eljay never loved me a-tall. Leroy don't care that much . . . El-jay . . . Beryl didn't care. But Kathie always be hurtin me the most. Nobody love me."

"Rainbow, she loves you in her way . . . as much as she can love anybody, she loves you."

"In her way? But her way don't weigh much. She sleeps with those men-friends she bring home. Likes goin out with them more than goin out with me. I hate myself for lovin her right on, no matter what she does. Kathie don't have much grace."

She stares straight into the candlelight and asks, "Miss Josie, did you take me in just to get paid more money for your bankbook? Did you? Or did you want . . . a friend?"

I no longer care to think up "proper" things to say. "It

was somewhat for money because I need money . . . but
I was interested or else I could not have done it."

"Miss Josie, do you love me?"

Her eyes hold me to *facts*. "I have grown to *care* about
you, Rainbow, truly I care . . . deeply."

"Will you please go to school with me and see Miss
Paloma and Miss Townes?"

"My pleasure."

Dishes in the sink now, blinds tilted against the morning sun. I place our case before her. "I've been thinking.
Let's ask Mayola to arrange for you to stay on here for
six months more . . . or so. Your mother could use some
time to get herself together. I need your company, also
could use the extra money. We might get along a lot
better than we have. I'll give you a birthday party. Can
have a party right here. Lotsa nice kids around, time you
branched out a little . . . with some new faces."

"I'll stay. You don't need to give a party. I wanta be
here. Kathie need to think and so do I. Sometime life
be that way."

17. RAINBOW

We walkin down the street. No matter what, feel like one somebody is in my corner. I told her when we left the house, "From now on, we not gonna view any more bodies, no matter who might die. We wanta live more lively. We not gonna die." I also told her, "I'm stayin away from canteen and the simpletons that hang out there . . . some of em ready to do the bump with whoever got a backside to bump against."

She try to jolly me along. "Canteen will look a lot better as time goes by. Eljay and Harold are not the only men in the world. And all of womanhood is not to be found in Miss Christopher and Janine."

"Yes, mam, like sometime I used to think that you, Miss Paloma and Miss Townes . . . and even Mrs. Anderson . . . tryin to act like yall better than anybody else. But all I say now is you gotta take people as individual."

"Rainey, I've been feeling like a complete failure. I'm going to learn how to consider myself in a better light."

"That's right, Miss Josie, let your light shine." Only light right now is the traffic and we waitin for it to turn green so we can get over to the other side.

"Rainey, I will utter one more lie, gladly. I'll tell the teachers that I am your *aunt* Josephine."

"No," I say. "Let's do it right. I'm tellin them you my friend who takes care of me cause my mother is away."

"That's just fine. Let's try truth. Mine will be facin up to my age."

"No," I say, "you bought eyelashes and face cream with *your* money. So do your thing and wear high heels, nice perfume and hair tint. Those kinda lies nothin but little ones. It's the big ones I'm gonna stop . . . like me tellin myself Kathie be gone cause-a her career or cause somebody is *makin* her do it. She gone cause that's what she wanta do . . . just like Mr. Harold and Eljay. They gone, gone, gone, while we standin round actin simple."

She stop, open her purse and take out a handkerchief. Her face is drippin sweat. She pattin face and neck dry. Maybe I hit her feelins all over again by mentionin Harold Lamont.

"You feel hot?" I ask.

"Yes Rainey," she say, "cause I'm on the last part of the change of life."

"Change-a life?"

"Yes, that time when the monthly period stops."

"You mean menopause?"

"That's right. I'm now finishing what you're just starting."

"Look to me like you'd be glad."

"I am, in one way of speaking."

"Wonder why it's call *men*-o-pause stead-a *women*-o-pause."

"Girl, you really make me laugh."

"Good, that shows we doin the best we can."

I'm feelin better walkin through the school corridor.
I'm holdin Miss Josie's arm. You never know, she might
get dizzy. I tell her . . . "I'm not scared bout nothin
Janine and that simple Eljay tell on me. Another thing,
if anybody ever ask me how old you are I'm gonna say
you forty-nine."

She laugh real good and say. "Thank you for *that*
lie." She look so happy, like wishin I was her daughter.
This lady really *need* somebody to help her out. One
solid truth is this . . . I don't want anybody to *ever* say
they love or even *care* about me if they don't really mean
it . . . and I promise to do them the same.

"Hold on, Miss Josie, stop and fresh up your lipstick
fore we go in to see Miss Paloma . . . so you be lookin
good."